MOSTLY RISKY

MOSTLY RISKY

HEATHER B.
MOORE

Mirror Press

Copyright © 2019 by Heather B. Moore
Print edition
All rights reserved

No part of this book may be reproduced in any form whatsoever without prior written permission of the publisher, except in the case of brief passages embodied in critical reviews and articles. This is a work of fiction. The characters, names, incidents, places, and dialogue are products of the author's imagination and are not to be construed as real.

Interior design by Cora Johnson
Edited by Kelsey Down, Lisa Shepherd, and Kimberley Montpetit
Cover design by Rachael Anderson and Steven Novak
Cover image credit: Deposit Photos #21975529

Published by Mirror Press, LLC
ISBN: 978-1-947152-92-2

The Women of Ambrose Estate

Mostly Dangerous
Mostly Perfect
Mostly Risky
Mostly Perilous

Amelia Ambrose's Genealogy

Ambrose Sisters:
Sofia
Lauren
Emma
Amelia
Kendra
Katelynn

Lauren's Parents:
Poppy Ambrose Chambers
Randall Aaron Chambers

Grandparents:
Lillian Marie Ambrose Millet
Richard Jacob Millet

Great-Grandparents
Helen Elizabeth Ambrose Burton
Walter Charles Burton

Great-Great-Grandparents
Margaret Florence Thorne Ambrose
George Frederick Ambrose II

All female descendants are given the extra middle name of Ambrose.

MOSTLY RISKY

A haunting curse. A voice from the past. A truth that will break her heart.

The Ambrose curse has stopped Amelia from following her heart. She's accepted her fate as part of the generations of Ambrose women who've lost their husbands too young. So Amelia is determined to never marry, to never allow herself to fall in love.

Grigg Edison has been patient long enough. Two years, in fact. When Amelia confesses that she's ready to test the power of the curse, all he wants is a chance. He'll do anything, including risking his heart in order to uncover the origin of the ancient legend.

But for Amelia, the risk may be too great, and the roots of family lore too deep.

1

AMELIA AMBROSE SCROLLED through her contacts, then wrote down five names. She took her time in writing each name, letting the memories wash over her. It was after hours in her office, so no one was about and no one would disturb her. No one would see her list. Ambrose & Edison Capital had cleared out for the night, so Amelia would have the place to herself until the janitorial service showed up around nine.

She traced the letters of the first name on her list again. Each of the men had been almost-boyfriends. Definitely at the top of her dating list. But for one reason or another, things hadn't quite worked out.

Okay. There was only *one* reason.

The curse that had plagued her family for generations, in which any man who married an Ambrose woman would meet an early death.

Truth really was stranger than fiction.

Back home, in Ambrose, Texas, were a half dozen graves to prove that the curse was real. Very real.

Yet now . . . two of her three older half sisters, Sofia and Lauren, had found a way to break the curse. For *them*. But broken all the same.

Amelia traced the second name again with her pen. She wished she knew what would break the curse for her. But her half sisters had been vague, saying something about giving up what she loved most.

Whatever that meant. They said she'd know it when she became serious about a guy.

She outlined the third name.

It was time. She was going to go for it. Pulling up the first name on the list, she pushed SEND on the phone contact. If Bryce still lived in Denver, then it was a good time to call. The phone rang once, then twice, and she imagined him grabbing his phone from wherever he'd set it in his home gym and seeing her name on the Caller ID. Did he still have her number? Or would it show up as *Unknown*?

Bryce was religious about working out and had the body to show for it. His workouts were twice a day. Once before his job as a patent lawyer began, and the second workout before the dinner hour, which for him was around 8:00 p.m. So right now was the best time to call him.

The phone clicked over to voicemail, and Amelia realized she hadn't counted the rings. Had he sent the call to voicemail? Or had it rung into voicemail?

When Bryce's recorded voice came on, Amelia found herself smiling at his upbeat tone. So like Bryce. She decided to leave a message. That's how serious she was about finding a boyfriend for real now.

"Hey, Bryce, it's Amelia Ambrose." She couldn't hold back a nervous half laugh. "I know. It's been a while. But you've popped into my mind a few times recently, and well, I wanted to check in. See how you're doing. My number's the same. Take care."

She'd done it. With a happy exhale, she clicked END on the phone.

"Wow," a deep voice said. "You called B Tots?"

Amelia yelped and placed her hand over her startled heart. Then she spun around in her swivel chair to see Grigg Edison leaning against the doorframe of her office, all long-legged, classic crooked smile, deep-brown eyes filled with their usual amusement.

"Grigg, I didn't hear you come in." Grigg was *the* Edison, as in the other half of Ambrose & Edison.

The edge of his mouth tugged up a bit more. "I'm like a panther, don't you know?"

She needed to hide her list. How could she do it without attracting Grigg's attention? He was the nosiest person in Colorado. He also said the most ridiculous things.

"Did you forget a report or something?" she asked in a nonchalant tone, despite the rapid thump of her heart.

"No." He scoffed. "You know I don't take home reports or anything else that resembles work."

It was true, and she was insanely jealous of that particular quality he had. She was always working, it seemed. Although, she was trying to change that. Beginning with finding a man to date whom she didn't have to break up with.

"So why are you here, Grigg?"

His half smile returned, and he scrubbed a hand through his dark hair that always managed to look groomed and charmingly disheveled at the same time. *Men.*

"I saw your light on my way back from dinner." He straightened and sauntered toward her. "It's late, Millie. Have you even eaten?"

No. And don't come any closer. She had to cover up the list. She turned her chair a bit and reached for the paper without looking at the desk and making it seem obvious.

But true to Grigg's observant nature, he noticed. And acted.

"What's this?" He stepped past her in a flash and snapped up the list. "You're making me another to-do list? . . . Oh . . ."

Amelia rose to her feet because that was the only way to contend with a six-foot-five guy like Grigg Edison. Who, by the way, had been the star quarterback at The Ohio State during his college years. Then had a late-season injury that put him out of the running for any NFL potential. He had refocused his education and gotten his MBA in finance. And now he ran the operations of their investment firm, and last year, she'd signed him on as partner.

She'd never regretted hiring the talented, sharp-witted finance whiz, until this moment.

"Please give it back, Grigg, it's nothing—"

"These are *all* guys you've dated," Grigg said, holding the list out of reach, which wasn't hard to do.

Amelia was only five foot six, something Grigg had teased her plenty about. That their heights were inversions of each other's. And she'd kicked off her high heels the moment the last person in the company had left for the night.

"Yeah, I know," she said, reaching again with a little hop this time. "I wrote the list. I think I know what's on it."

Grigg stepped back, but Amelia followed. She grabbed his other arm and tugged him toward her, which wasn't easy, since he might be lean, but he was also strong.

"Bryce, Clint, Hayden . . ." He was literally dragging her with him as he backpedaled. "Peter? *Jack?* What are you up to, Mills?"

She both hated and loved it when Grigg called her Mills. As far as nicknames went, it was pretty basic, but it also told people they were close friends. On the other hand, she wanted to be respected in the finance industry, not only as a businesswoman but as a successful executive. And not be teased by her partner.

"Grigg, give me that list."

He stilled.

She'd used her mom voice. Or at least what he'd called her mom voice. Usually he'd laugh, but somehow, thankfully, he didn't now.

"Here." He lowered his arm and handed her the list. Then he folded those well-sculpted arms of his. "Spill, cuz. You know I'm not going to be happy if you hook up with any of them. Especially B Tots."

List in hand, Amelia's rising panic began to dissipate. *Cuz* was another name he'd adopted for her. A few months into their working relationship, a couple of their clients had asked if they were boyfriend-girlfriend. No. Not even close. Griggs had blurted out that they were cousins. Later, he had told her that of course they were cousins. Probably eight or ten times removed, but still cousins.

But the nickname had worked in their favor in more than one situation. It stopped any gossip or speculation about a man and woman who worked so closely together and were both still unattached. Which Amelia could now remedy on her side of things.

"*Bryce* being allergic to potatoes, or more specifically tater tots, is not something you should make fun of."

"I stand by my original assessment," Griggs said, leaning against her desk so that he was still in her space. He was good at that. Getting into her space until he got the answers he was seeking. Whether it be with work life or personal life. "I've never heard of a person being allergic to tater tots, but not other types of potatoes."

"It's the spice, I guess," she said, "or the way they're created at the manufacturing plant. I don't know, and it doesn't concern you."

At this, his brows arched. She'd seen that expression before. Many times. In fact, she knew all of Grigg Edison's expressions. All his moods. What made him laugh. What made him angry. What made him leave the office at 6:00 p.m. sharp every night and arrive the next morning at 7:45 a.m.

"Mills . . . you're wounding me."

His hand on his heart was so dramatic, and if Amelia had been in a better mood, she might have laughed. But she hadn't wanted this interruption. She hadn't wanted anyone to see her list.

She tucked the list into her bag, then proceeded to power down her laptop, unplug the cord, and load everything up.

"Hey, I'm sorry."

His voice was low, deep, and sincere. She looked up at him, into those dark-brown eyes of his that many women swooned over. Thing was, Grigg didn't really date. Well, he dated, but not anyone long-term. Said he'd had a serious relationship the last couple of years in college, but the woman had ditched him when he'd gotten injured. Apparently she'd wanted to be an NFL player's wife.

"Sit down," she said with a sigh. "I have something to tell you."

2

GRIGG WASN'T ABOUT to turn down Amelia's order to sit, but he was leery all the same. He couldn't believe he'd walked in on her calling an old boyfriend. Well, *boyfriend* was too strong of a word. Amelia Ambrose believed she was cursed and could never be in a serious relationship, or get married for that matter.

She'd told him all about her deep-rooted Texan family, her billionaire grandmother, and the family curse one night when they'd both come into work over the weekend. She'd told him how the Ambrose family property covered about fifteen thousand acres to run cattle and produce oil. Her grandmother had kept the business running after her husband died young in the 1950s.

It seemed that Amelia had inherited her grandmother's love for running a business and spending all hours to do it. Working weekends was a rarity for Grigg, but a commonality for Amelia.

Grigg had learned to listen to his body after spending his entire life, starting at age ten, playing football. There had been no rest, ever. And when he'd torn every ligament in his knee with two games to go in his college football career, he'd gone through physical and emotional hell for six months.

He'd also learned that there was more to life outside of nonstop, high-level achievement. The world of finance had been something to occupy his mind and give him new goals, ones that didn't start at the crack of dawn lifting weights and end at midnight in an ice bath.

Now he lived by the clock in a different way. His work had a definite starting and ending time each day.

Grigg sat in the chair next to Amelia's desk. She remained standing for a moment, as if she were unsure of how to begin. This was intriguing. Amelia Ambrose wasn't usually at a loss for words, but he'd noticed the higher pitch in her voice and the flush of her cheeks when he'd snatched the list from her desktop.

"Don't tell me, you found a way to break the Ambrose curse," he joked.

But she didn't laugh. In fact, her dark-blue eyes were as serious as he'd ever seen them. Some women enhanced their beauty with makeup. Amelia needed no makeup as far as he was concerned. Early in their career together, he had found himself coming into the office on weekends, not to work but to see her. Because that was when she dressed in jeans and wore her black hair in a messy ponytail. Sans makeup. Beautiful.

Then she had told him about the Ambrose curse and how there was no future for her with any man. Which included him, of course. Not that he'd been crushing on her. No, he respected her as a colleague too much for that. Okay, he'd been crushing on her, and he likely still was, he guessed. In a completely arms-length sort of way. He hadn't dated anyone seriously since working with Amelia, and yeah, he'd used his college breakup as an excuse, but it wasn't the full reason.

So he'd stopped coming to the office on the weekends, because truthfully it was too hard to be around her one-on-one when her guard was down. When her smiles and laughter were unchecked and unfettered. When it was just the two of them, for hours and hours—working, yes, but also talking and teasing.

"I've told you about my older sisters, well, half sisters, right?"

"Right," Grigg said, eying her. "Sofia, Lauren, and Emma?"

She nodded, seeming pleased he'd remembered their names.

Of course he remembered. It being a Thursday night, she was still wearing one of her power suits, and although she'd ditched her high heels somewhere, she still looked the part of a composed businesswoman. Except for when she'd been trying to wrestle the list away from him.

Her mascara was a bit smudged, and she'd tugged out whatever updo she'd worn that day, so her dark hair tumbled about her shoulders. This was a look he wouldn't ever complain about.

"I talked to each of them tonight," Amelia continued. "I know. I'm not the best sister in the world, and tonight must have been a record. But there've been some things going on among the Ambrose women lately that caught my attention."

Grigg leaned forward and rested his forearms on his knees. "Such as?"

She bit the edge of her lip, a sure sign that she was hesitant about something. "Well, both Sofia and Lauren have discovered how to break the curse."

Well. This was unexpected. He liked that her dark eyes gleamed with excitement, but if there truly was a curse at all, how could they really know? Unless her sisters married and their husbands didn't die in the next five to ten years.

She lifted her hand. "I know, I know what you're thinking, but it's true. Although I don't know exactly how I'll break the curse over me personally, since they all said that I'll know it when I'm with the right man. The man I fall in love with, that is."

Grigg swallowed the pebbles that had suddenly lodged in his throat. "Thus, the list of five potentials?"

Her smile was slow, but genuine. "Exactly."

"Can I see it again?" he asked.

This time she didn't hesitate, since apparently confessing had made her more eager to share. She dug the paper out of her laptop bag and handed it over. Grigg scanned the list, if only to give himself something to do while his thoughts jumbled and separated and jumbled again. He probably read over the names a dozen times, maybe even two dozen times, before he lifted his gaze to meet Amelia's anticipated one. He had met four of the five men on the list while she had been dating them. The only one he didn't recognize was Hayden, but with a name like that Grigg was pretty sure he didn't need to meet the guy. Hayden would be an automatic cross off.

"So," Grigg began in a slow tone, "you call each of these guys and tell them, 'Sorry for breaking up with you, but I'm now available because I know you won't die if we get married'?"

Amelia's face flushed a pretty pink. "Not in those words exactly. But that's the gist of it."

"Wow, Mills, that's all so . . . *clinical.*"

She looked away and bit her lip again.

Grigg knew he should feel bad about the tone of his voice, which definitely had an edge to it. But he didn't want to see Amelia throwing herself at anyone, let alone to any of those five names on her list. None of which Grigg had been particularly impressed with. Not that Amelia had asked his opinion on any of them when she dated them. And he wasn't her older brother or her true cousin. But they were friends nonetheless, right?

He'd given her dating advice, and she'd given him dating advice. Of course his dating advice to her never went anywhere, because she would only date for a few weeks, maybe a couple months, and then as things started to get a little serious, she'd bail. As far as Grigg went, he mostly *pretended* he was dating longer than he actually was. Sure, he'd go out with a woman once, maybe twice, and end things before he told Amelia they were over. He didn't want her to think he was a playboy. Because he was far from that. He was a one-woman kind of guy. And had been for the past two years. The problem was, the woman he was most interested in on this planet wouldn't even consider going out with him on a single date.

Right now, it seemed that the floodgates were about to open for Amelia's dating life, starting with this list. Grigg couldn't really believe that one of these five men had the potential to be Amelia's happily ever after. Of course he could be wrong, but if her mind frame had changed about dating in general, then what opportunities might befall her out there, beyond the glass windows of this office building? He'd seen her flirt. He'd seen her turn down offers of lunch, offers of dinner, offers of drinks. Some of them from their own clients. Some of them at meet and greets, socials, events, or conferences. He'd seen her hold back when she was interested in getting to know a man better, and he'd seen her hesitation over and over. Yeah, he felt sorry for her. But really, he felt selfish. Because the longer she didn't date anyone else, the longer he could have her to himself. Even though their relationship had only been in the friend zone.

Right now, he found himself between a rock and a hard place. Amelia was about to go out there into the Wild West of dating. Did she even have dating apps on her phone? Amelia Ambrose was beautiful, talented, witty . . . Did he mention beautiful? Oh, and she was also filthy rich. If this had been the 19th century she would have been possibly the most eligible woman in the country. The only other exceptions would have been the rest of the Ambrose sisters, none of whom Grigg had had the opportunity to meet yet. But by listening to a dozen stories, he had learned enough about the savvy, smart women to know that if they were even one-tenth the quality of Amelia, they were also dynamic catches. Any man would be fortunate to be part of their lives.

Grigg exhaled. He had the feeling that he needed to tread carefully. If Amelia was set on this course, then he knew more than anyone else that she would head down it. She might have had plenty of seed money to start this investment firm, but it was her intellect that kept it running successfully.

So if he tried to stop her or discourage her, then she would separate from him. And not include him in her personal affairs again. But if Grigg was supportive, could he stand to watch her make these phone calls, report back about her dates, and possibly fall in love?

"Hey," Grigg said in a soft voice. "I'm just, uh, surprised you'd want to see B Tots again. I mean, doesn't that guy drink spinach juice for breakfast?"

The edge of her mouth lifted.

"But hey, if it's Popeye you want, then maybe we could go out on a double date or something," Grigg said. *Where is this coming from?* The last thing he wanted was a front-row seat to Amelia's dating life. But then again, that was exactly what he wanted. He wanted to be with her every chance he got. Even if it meant on a double date. It seemed he was a glutton for punishment. Because the answer was *yes*: he wanted to stay in the passenger seat, next to Amelia's life, for as long as he could.

"A double date, huh?" she asked, her smile returning.

Grigg's heart might have betrayed him and flipped a time or two. "Yep. That's what I said."

"So you can give me your opinion after the date?" she said. "Let me know if you approve?"

Grigg leaned back in his chair. He stretched out his legs in front of him and crossed his ankles. Then he said in the most nonchalant way possible, "Yeah, I figure we're pretty good friends. We've been working together a long time. And I might know a little something about who would make you happy. And what would make you happy. So I could meet up with you guys with my own date. And then after, we can see if B Tots stays on your list."

"And what about the other guys?" she said, her blue eyes the color of a mountain lake.

Grigg merely tilted his head and smiled. "I'm all in, cuz."

Amelia laughed, and Grigg ignored the rush of warmth in his veins. "I think in this case," she said, "acting like we're cousins will be to our advantage."

Grigg smiled, because really it was against what he wanted to do. He wasn't sure exactly what he had just gotten himself into. What he had just committed to. He just hoped he wouldn't regret it.

3

BRYCE CALLED AMELIA back at 10:00 p.m. She was both surprised and pleased. Once Grigg left the office earlier that night, Amelia had battled between feeling like a fool and feeling a strange sense of excitement. Was her life really going to move to the next level? She was only twenty-four, but she'd already reconciled herself to living like her sisters. Single. Single. Single. But now, Amelia had two half sisters who had found men to love and to love them in return.

"Amelia!" Bryce said the second she answered. "It's been a really long time. How are you?"

Amelia turned off the television. She hadn't been watching the latest Netflix series anyway; it was just background noise as she prepared for a meeting with a new client tomorrow. Bateson Cupcakes had sent over their financials, and she wanted to become familiar with them so that their meeting would be as productive as possible.

"Bryce," she said, keeping her tone light, casual. "How are you? Thanks for calling back. I know this is sort of out of the blue." She laughed, hoping that Bryce would join her. He did.

"Yeah, you did surprise me, I gotta admit." He paused. "You still in the Denver area? Financing one entrepreneur at a time?"

"Something like that." She smiled. It was great to hear Bryce's voice. His tone was low and warm, and she'd forgotten how much she loved talking to him during the late nights when they were both winding down from busy days. In fact, ten o'clock was sort of like *their* time. Ironic now. "I'm still in Denver. Most days."

"A woman always on the run," he said, and she heard the smile in his voice. "So what's new with you?"

In other words, he wanted to know why she called him. It was a fair question. So she dove right in. "Business is about the same. Busy as usual. But, like I said in my message, you've been on my mind for some reason. And I realize now that I probably ended things between us before I really gave you a chance. I guess I regret it."

Bryce didn't say anything, and Amelia worried she might have made a huge mistake.

"Sorry, that was pretty bold of me. I mean, you might have a girlfriend." She closed her eyes and exhaled. "Heck, you might be engaged. Or even married?" She left it as a question because he still wasn't speaking.

Another awkward silence.

"Look, Amelia," Bryce said at last, "you're a great woman. Beautiful. Of course you know that, since I used to tell you all the time. But I'm getting the feeling that you're in a tough spot for whatever reason, and you think I'm going to bail you out. Maybe fill in some lonely hours that you're experiencing. But honestly, I'm pretty happy where I'm at right now. And yeah, I am dating someone, but it's just the beginning. So nothing serious right now."

Amelia's face was surely bright red. Her stomach turned, and she felt like she wouldn't mind being swallowed up by the floor right about now. Was it possible to rewind time, for even five minutes? Was that too hard to ask with all the scientific advances in the world? There were movies about time machines. What were they based on? Science? Or imagination? And now she had to backtrack. Big time.

"I'm not surprised," she said. "Not surprised at all. I mean, you're a great guy, Bryce. Always were. I'm glad we talked, and please know that I wish you all the best, whether dating this woman turns into something more or you end up meeting someone else special down the road." Was her voice shaky now too? Had Bryce noticed? Was she going to cry?

"Thanks, Amelia." His tone sounded resigned. "It's great to hear from you as well. And honestly, I'm glad you called. I think about you sometimes too, and I won't deny that I kind of wondered if things would have been different between us, if . . . Well, you know."

"If I hadn't ghosted you," Amelia finished. "Well, you'll be glad to know that I've matured a little. Hopefully for the better."

Bryce chuckled. "I don't think you were immature. I think you were looking for something else. *Someone* else. And I don't take any offense to that. The attraction has to be mutual."

"Lack of attraction wasn't ever the problem between us," Amelia said. "Believe me. You're a beautiful person too. Thanks for everything, Bryce."

When they finally hung up, Amelia didn't feel like she was going to cry anymore. The nervous shaking had stopped, and in fact, she was a bit relieved. Bryce was a nice guy; he was a great guy. And he'd moved on. That was what was supposed to happen. People break up, and people move on. That was the healthy thing to do.

She picked up the list of five names. Bryce had been at the top, and now she'd cross him off. She leaned her head back on the couch, closed her eyes, and thought about the next name on her list. Clint. He traveled frequently to the East Coast, so if he was there, it would be pretty late. And a midnight phone call wouldn't be welcome, even though he was a baseball junkie and was likely watching some late baseball game right now. She also knew enough not to disturb him while he watched baseball, unless she wanted to talk about the game.

Well, being a workaholic didn't exactly earn a girl a lot of friends. So instead of calling a girlfriend and talking about the embarrassing phone call with Bryce, she called Grigg. It seemed he was the next best thing.

The phone had already rung twice before she realized maybe she shouldn't be calling Grigg at this time of night. It wasn't too long after ten, but it was still late by any casual standards. Definitely too late for a work call. Of course Grigg knew her schedule, which was pretty much *work anytime night or day*. Still. She was about to hang up when she heard his voice.

"Hey, Mills," Grigg answered. "What did B Tots say?"

"*Bryce*. And how do you know I already talked to him?" Amelia asked.

"I'm just *that* good," Grigg said. "Either that or I put two and two together."

"And what would that be?"

"First of all, you're calling me after ten." She heard something rustle. A wrapper? Had he been eating? Was he even alone?

"And what's the second thing?" she prompted.

"Even though I don't exactly approve of B Tots, I seriously doubt he would have waited more than a couple hours to call you back." Grigg chuckled. "I mean, he *is* a man, and you *are* a beautiful woman."

Now, Amelia didn't think twice about Grigg calling her beautiful. Giving compliments was part of his language. He said a lot of nice things to a lot of people, including herself. And yes, he'd called her beautiful plenty of times. In fact, that used to be one of his nicknames for her, until she had put a firm stop to it.

"It seems you're right on both counts." She shifted on the couch and pulled her feet up.

"Then don't hold me in suspense, cuz. What's the time and place of our double date? And do you think if I wore a suit, it would be too much?"

Amelia laughed. Grigg only wore a suit when absolutely required. In fact he had lobbied for a company rule to have all client meetings on Mondays and Tuesdays, which would mean that the rest of the week he could wear his khakis and button-down shirts. That had not gotten approved, and it wasn't because Amelia had wanted to vote no. It was because her company accepted most walk-in clients, and some of those turned into impromptu meetings with either her or Grigg.

After all, their firm had a reputation to uphold. Efficient, professional, and fair.

"Here's the thing," Amelia said. "Bryce is dating someone, so I pretty much made a fool out of myself."

"Oh."

"Is that all you're going to say?" Amelia asked.

"I think I am speechless," Grigg said, his voice sounding strangely like he was trying not to laugh.

"Laughing at me is not considered speechless," Amelia said. "I mean, it was an honest mistake."

"I'm not laughing at *you*, Mills," Grigg said. "At least not in the way you think I am."

The thing with Grigg was that it was hard not to smile when he laughed. He had one of those deep, rumbling, contagious laughs. Despite herself, a smile crept its way onto her face.

"And for the record, cuz, whatever B Tots has going on, he's missing out by turning you down."

"Has anyone ever told you that you'd make a good mom?"

Grigg didn't hide his laughter now. It was a running joke between them. Whenever they were either annoyed at each other or wanting to give a backhanded compliment, they brought in the mom card.

"Why? Because I'm trying to make you feel better?"

"Yes, exactly. *Mom*."

"Well, if moms speak the truth, then I'll own the title," he said. "Maybe I should start wearing a T-shirt about how awesome moms are."

Amelia snickered. "I'm not going to dare you to do it, because somehow I think you would."

"It seems you make me do a lot of things I normally would not," Grigg said. "Such as going on a double date. Who's up next on your list? Hayden?"

"No, Clint."

"Ah, Mr. Baseball Stats," Grigg said in a smooth tone. "Think he could work you in? I mean, it's the middle of the season."

He was right, but still. "Lunch date?"

Grigg's laughter was warm, reaching through the phone like a friendly hug. "Mills, these men won't know what's hit them. I feel sorry for the poor sap whose heart is going to get broken next."

Amelia straightened up at this. "What do you mean? I'm totally open to a relationship with one of them. These are my top five ever. Well, top four now. But no one's heart is going to get broken, because I'm a new woman now."

"Not to disagree," Grigg said, "but you're the same Amelia with or without the curse hanging over you. You have to admit that if you'd really fallen in love with one of them, you would have found a way to make it work no matter what. I mean, you're Amelia Ambrose, founder of one of the most prestigious investment firms in Denver. Heck, maybe the entire nation."

"Easy, Grigg," she said. "I forgot how grandiose you get after your bedtime."

"Babe, you haven't seen anything yet."

Amelia's breath stalled. *Babe.* That was a new one. She should ignore it. Move on. She had to think of something, and quick, because she didn't like the goose bumps spreading across her arms one bit. "Tell me who *your* date's going to be? That Melanie woman?"

"Melanie?" His tone sounded confused.

"The blond?"

"Oh, she's, uh, out of the picture," he said. "But don't worry, I'll find someone, and she'll probably be a huge baseball nut too. Then you and I can eat their dessert on the sly while they talk about batting averages."

Amelia giggled. Which told her she was getting too tired to keep up the banter with Grigg. "Sounds like a plan."

When she hung up with Grigg, Amelia stared at nothing for several moments. Tomorrow she hoped the embarrassment of calling Bryce would fade. But tonight she was going to have to live with it. At least she was no longer in this alone.

4

IT TURNED OUT that getting a date at the last minute was not so difficult after all. Grigg had simply asked Maggie on his usual coffee run to Starbucks if she had any lunch plans later that day. He knew she only worked as a barista in the mornings, because she was also a grad student at the University of Denver.

"Is three o'clock your usual lunch hour?" Grigg asked while they walked together to the restaurant that was down the block from the coffee shop.

"Fridays I don't have classes," Maggie said. She was about two inches shorter than Grigg. Apparently she had been a volleyball player all through college. So at six foot three she was perhaps the tallest woman he'd ever dated.

Well, *dated* was not quite the right word. Because this was going to be a one-and-done date. He just hoped that she wouldn't mess up on his coffee the next time he came in when he didn't ask her out again.

So here they were, walking to the Italian café where Amelia and Clint would be meeting them.

Truthfully, Grigg was relieved that Bryce had been crossed off the list already. In physical looks, Bryce was hard for any man to compete with. Not that Grigg had a low self-esteem or anything; even he thought Bryce was good-looking. But thankfully, he'd turned Amelia down flat, so only four more were left in the running. Four more to convince to cross off her list.

"So how's work at your firm going?" Maggie asked.

"Busy as usual," Grigg said, "but things are going well." This might be a long lunch, since he and Maggie really knew very little about each other, so it would be awkward if they were talking about basics like number of siblings, favorite color, and favorite foods on a double date.

Whereas, with Clint and Amelia, they were already past that stage, or at least they had been when they'd been dating.

"Do you like baseball?" Grigg asked.

Maggie scrunched up her nose. "I don't *not* like it," she said. "I mean, my brothers played in high school, but they never went past that. I watched their games, when I wasn't doing volleyball stuff, of course."

"Cool." They'd arrived at the restaurant, and since there was no sign of Amelia and her date outside, Grigg opened the door for Maggie to pass through. "Amelia's date is a big baseball fan, so I'm sure that will become a topic of conversation during our lunch." Might as well give her a small warning.

Grigg saw Amelia first, and it looked like Clint had shown up and was on time. Amelia wore one of her usual power suits. This one was a pale gray, with a blue blouse, coupled with high heels. He wondered if anyone else in their firm knew how often she kicked off those heels when she was sitting at her desk. Sometimes he teased her about it, asking her why she didn't wear flats like some of the other women. But she'd given him one of her scowling looks. He'd laughed and dropped the subject.

Now she turned, as if she sensed them walking in. Grigg noticed right away that she'd done up her makeup more than usual. She also wore earrings, which wasn't all that unusual, and her heart-shaped pendant. She'd told him that her grandmother had given her the pendant on her sixteenth birthday, calling it the Pendant of Protection. The inscription inside the heart read *Together We Are Strong.*

Grigg knew for a fact that Amelia never took it off; it was one of her superstitions and connected to her family curse.

But now that she knew the curse could be broken, would she take it off? Apparently his mind could get quite distracted when he was thinking about Amelia, even when she was standing in front of him. Her dark-blue gaze held a question, and he realized that she had just spoken, but he'd totally missed it.

"Hi, Amelia," he said, ignoring her confused gaze. "Nice to see you again, Clint."

The blond man shook Grigg's hand. It was a very brief handshake. And one that was a bit sweaty. Clint was the kind of guy who never sat still, never stopped moving, like he was always ready to spring. Like he couldn't hold back his energy. As introductions were made all around, it seemed that Clint was ready to bolt at any minute.

Was the guy nervous? Then Grigg noticed that Clint kept looking at another table about halfway into the restaurant. Did he know someone that he didn't want to see?

The waitress led them to their table, and they passed by the couple that Clint had been eyeing. The woman seated at the table flushed, and Grigg went on alert. Obviously there was something going on between Clint and that woman, or at the very least they had a past together.

Not that it was Grigg's business—but if Amelia started to really like Clint, then it would become everyone's business.

As they sat down, Grigg sneaked another glance at the woman Clint had noticed. She wore a wedding ring, and the man she was sitting with also wore a wedding ring. Which meant that most likely they were a married couple. The plot had just thickened.

Grigg didn't have to contribute much to the conversation after all; no, he just had to sit back while the other three talked baseball. Maggie *did* know quite a bit about baseball, and for all intents and purposes she acted like she was still a fan. What she didn't know about the pro teams, Clint was clearly happy to fill her in.

Everyone ordered, and Grigg decided to go out on a limb and order the lasagna. Amelia immediately noticed. "You're not getting your usual chicken fettuccine Alfredo?" she asked.

Clint's gaze swung in Grigg's direction. Maggie raised her brows.

Well, now that Grigg had everyone's attention, he guessed he should explain. "I feel like trying something new today, that's all."

"Do you always order the same thing when you go out to eat?" Maggie said.

"Always," Amelia deadpanned. "Grigg orders chicken fettuccine Alfredo at any Italian restaurant, chicken massaman when we eat Thai food, chicken enchiladas with green enchilada sauce when we eat Mexican—"

"I don't think they want to hear all my secrets," Grigg cut in with a laugh.

Amelia smirked.

"I guess you two eat out a lot together?" Maggie asked, her brows raised.

Clint's eyes had narrowed.

Ah. Grigg could see how this all sounded. Perhaps that wouldn't be a bad thing for Clint, but Grigg didn't want Maggie to think he was a two-timing jerk.

"Work lunches," Amelia said.

"Yep," Grigg said. "Since Amelia doesn't eat dinner, it's all about the work lunches, provided of course there really is work being discussed."

Another smirk from Amelia.

"How long have you guys been working together?" Maggie looked back and forth between them.

"Two years," they both said at once.

Grigg reached for his ice water and took a long swallow.

Miraculously, and thankfully, Maggie said, "It must be nice to work with a cousin."

Right . . . perfect segue. "Yeah, it is great," he said. "Like a family connection, but without the sibling rivalry."

Maggie laughed. She was a pretty woman, a different pretty than Amelia. But Grigg could appreciate more than one type of woman. Maybe this wouldn't be their one and only date.

But then Clint turned the tables.

"What do *you* do, Maggie?" he asked.

Grigg was surprised at Clint's pointed interest in Maggie, then he noticed that the couple with the wedding rings had left their table. Now Clint's attention wasn't divided any longer.

She talked about her job as a barista, then her graduate work in psychology and child development. And wouldn't you know, Clint found it fascinating. Who would have thought that a baseball nut would be so interested in Maggie's social work? And honestly, Grigg was impressed too. Both with Maggie's work commitment and the fact that they were no longer talking about baseball.

By the end of lunch, Grigg estimated that Maggie and Clint had talked the most to each other. Which was completely fine with him, but was it fine with Amelia? He tried to catch her gaze more than once, to assess her internal thoughts about how the date was going with Clint, but she wasn't meeting Grigg's eyes. In fact, she was sneaking plenty of glances at her phone. Maybe her attention had already been diverted back to work.

As the four of them walked out of the restaurant together, sure enough Amelia said something about hurrying back to work. The comment was lost on Clint and Maggie—because Maggie was currently telling Clint about the case study she was working on, and Clint had apparently been through the foster system when he was a kid. So it was that Grigg and Amelia walked back to their office together, leaving their dates still talking outside of the restaurant.

"What just happened?" Amelia asked.

"I think we both got ditched," Grigg said. "I thought baseball was going to dominate, but apparently it was social work."

"I thought Maggie looked familiar," Amelia said. "Have you had your eye on her for a while?"

"Not exactly," Grigg said.

Amelia seemed surprised at that. "So this was your first date?"

"Yep. And I think it was our last," Grigg said.

Amelia slowed her step as they reached their building. Grigg slowed too and looked down at her.

"Did you ask her out because you like her? Or because we had planned this double date?"

Grigg smiled. "A man's gotta have at least one secret."

Amelia folded her arms. And kept watching him. Well, if Grigg had her undivided attention, maybe he could give her a little information. He couldn't fathom how Clint could have passed up a woman like Amelia for anyone, even Maggie. "Alright, you caught me. I did ask Maggie out for this lunch because of the double date. She's a nice girl, and I knew that she wouldn't be a poor choice. But I also didn't want her to read into things too much. I already knew going into it that it would be a one-day thing. Clint saved me the trouble. Such a gentleman."

Amelia's mouth turned up at the corners as if she was pleased, or triumphant. It was hard to tell.

"You satisfied now?" Grigg asked. "Maybe *I* should make a list, one that will match up with yours."

"You know you don't have to come on every date with me," she said. "I mean, I think the date with Hayden is going to be really painful for you. You've already made fun of his name."

"Have you called him yet?" Grigg asked. "We getting together for Hawaiian haystacks?"

Amelia shoved his arm. "I was waiting to see how things with Clint went."

Grigg nodded. "And how do you think things went?" He tried to hide his smirk but failed.

Amelia looked heavenward. "Well, you were there, and I agree with you. We both got ditched."

"I guess we won't know for sure until Clint calls to tell you the bad news."

Amelia shrugged. "I don't think Clint's gonna call me. He's more like the blow-me-off type of person. At least that's what happened last time we dated."

Now this was new to Grigg. "Really?"

"Why does that surprise you?" she asked.

"Because," he said in a slow voice, focusing on her blue eyes, "you've always been the heartbreaker in your relationships."

"Not always," she said. "Clint stopped reaching out to me when I canceled two dates in a row. They were real excuses too, not *me* blowing *him* off."

Grigg slipped his hands into his pockets because the wind had picked up and he was tempted to move back the flyaway strands of hair from her cheek. "So we're onto number three. Are you calling Hayden tonight?"

Amelia smiled. "Yep. There's no reason to waste any time."

No reason at all.

5

AMELIA SMILED TO herself as she approached Hayden at the French café where they'd agreed to meet. His profile told her he hadn't changed at all from the always-in-need-of-a-haircut professor type. When Amelia had first met Hayden a while back at a mutual friend's wedding, he'd reminded her a bit of her father. Both were highly intelligent and worked in the field of academics.

Amelia's father was her mother's second husband, and Poppy had told Amelia more than once that she'd wanted to marry a man who wasn't a daredevil pilot. Amelia's dad had been a professor of science with a bit of an obsessive personality—similar to Hayden in a way but completely different in looks. Amelia never saw her father without his pristinely clean clothing and hair buzzed short. Hayden always wore a slightly rumpled button-down shirt with a bow tie, along with khakis worn at the hems.

Still, just because her father wasn't an air force pilot didn't mean that his death hadn't come early. Because of the curse. Now Amelia blinked away memories of her father and refocused on the history professor she was about to have a meal with. Hayden was only a couple of inches taller than her, and he wore a button-down, plaid shirt, khakis, and his usual scruffy, longish hair, and round glasses.

When Hayden's light-blue eyes landed on her, she felt gratified at the warmth in them.

"Amelia, it's great to see you," he said. He leaned down and kissed her cheek, which she didn't necessarily mind, but it felt new.

Hayden hadn't been the most affectionate man to date. Yes, they'd held hands and kissed a few times, but he always seemed more interested in ruminating about things long in the past.

"Great to see you too." Amelia straightened her blazer. She hadn't had time to go home and change, since a meeting had gone longer than usual. In fact, she'd left Grigg to finish it up, which probably meant he and his date would be a no-show tonight. Amelia had no doubt that Grigg would just take Silvia to another place later.

Amelia didn't want to think about Silvia right now, or Grigg and Silvia . . . She was a beautiful and sweet woman who worked at the after-hours call center for their building. Grigg had said that Silvia wouldn't read much into the dinner invitation, but Amelia had seen the way the woman checked out Grigg. Whatever happened was fine. Grigg didn't even like French food, and he'd asked Amelia if she could change the restaurant location. She'd laughed and told him no. After all, it wasn't a date with Grigg but with Hayden.

"Our table is ready," Hayden said. "I'll let the hostess know that you've arrived."

"Okay, thanks."

Moments later, Amelia was sitting across from Hayden at a circular booth. On the table, small candles glowed among the crystal wine glasses and fine china. Low classical music played, and this place would be plenty romantic if she were here with someone she was in love with.

Was Hayden a possibility? He'd opened the menu as soon as they were seated, and now he was mouthing the menu items, in French no less.

Amelia cracked hers open. She understood enough French from taking it in high school to get the gist of most of the dishes. But she was no connoisseur. She'd stick with chicken and some sort of sauce.

"We should order the oysters for an appetizer," Hayden said, looking up at her. "They're very good here."

Amelia didn't love oysters, but she didn't hate them either. "Sounds good."

"In fact, let me order the rest of your meal," Hayden said. "I'll surprise you."

She didn't really like the idea, but the hopeful look on Hayden's face changed her mind. "If you insist."

He reached for her hand, another surprise in the affection department. "I do insist." He gave a soft laugh. "I let you get away once, and I don't plan to again. I've learned that I need to be more assertive with women, ask for what I want. Find better ways to meet their needs."

Okay, then, she thought. Was this all a good thing or a bad thing?

The waitress took their order, which Hayden delivered completely in French.

Amelia was impressed, although she was probably overanalyzing things too much. Whenever she'd dated in the past, she knew she was only dating for the short term and not to find a husband. So this felt different. Which probably was making her more hyperaware.

After the waitress left with a promise to bring their hors d'oeuvres soon, Amelia asked, "How is the university these days? Are you teaching a full class load again?"

Hayden smiled. "I'm teaching four undergraduate classes and two graduate classes. I'm also on the committee for historical preservation at the university. Keeps me almost as busy as you. Although I won't ever be in your income bracket, I'm happy."

Amelia smiled to hide the prickle of irritation that climbed along her neck. "Sounds like you're doing great things. Have you published any articles lately?"

"I have." Hayden proceeded to fill her in, almost word for word, about an article he had written about the turn-of-the-century conflicts that led to World War I.

She tried to focus, she really did, but her mind kept straying to the meeting she'd left Grigg to finish up. How were things going, and would he follow through with the recommendations they'd discussed together? What about—

"Hello there. Sorry we're late."

Amelia snapped her head up to see Grigg standing before their table, with Silvia at his side.

"Did you order yet?" Grigg asked. "We can call the waitress back over and be quick about it."

Hayden's eyes about popped open.

Amelia recovered first. "It's only been a few minutes. I'm sure they can get yours in too. Uh, Hayden, this is my business partner, Grigg Edison."

"Nice to meet you." He stuck out his hand, and Hayden half rose to shake it. "And this is Silvia."

"Hello there." Silvia wore a formfitting black dress, covered in sequins no less, and she definitely had plenty of curves to show off. Her blond hair and smoky eyes would draw any man, and Amelia didn't miss Hayden's appreciative gaze.

Maybe Amelia should have brought extra clothing to the office, since she was feeling like a stuffed suit in this scenario.

Grigg had even dressed down somehow. Yeah, he was still wearing the same pants and shirt as he had at the office. But he'd ditched his tie, unbuttoned a couple of shirt buttons, rolled up his sleeves, and looked relaxed and casual. And sexy. Amelia bit her lip. Where had that thought come from?

Grigg motioned Silvia toward the booth, but she shook her head. "You first. I want to be on the end, in case I need to visit the powder room."

Grigg didn't make any effort to protest, and instead, he slid in right next to Amelia.

She scooted over, and so did Hayden, but she was effectively sandwiched between both men.

This close to Grigg, she could smell his light spice, whereas Hayden smelled faintly of paper, if she were to make an assessment.

"Oysters, huh?" Grigg said.

The waitress had arrived and set down a large platter with a dozen oysters artfully arranged on ice.

"They're excellent here," Hayden said. "Please help yourself."

"I've never tried oysters," Silvia said. "Aren't they cold and slimy?"

Hayden chuckled. "They are that, but so much more as well." He then proceeded to show her how to prepare the oysters for eating.

Silvia picked one up and followed Hayden's direction. Then she downed the thing.

"Oh," she said, her eyes widening. "Not bad, but strange."

Hayden looked pleased, and Amelia frowned as she looked between him and Silvia. Would this be another date swap?

"What about you, Grigg?" Hayden asked. "Are you going to have one? You don't want to leave your date hanging, do you?"

"Oh, sure. I'll try one," Grigg said.

Amelia hid a smirk. His tone was less enthusiastic. She watched him gingerly pick up the oyster, prepare it, then swallow it down.

She was pretty sure his normally tanned skin lost some color.

Grigg reached for her water and, without asking her, drank from it.

"Good, huh?" Hayden said.

Grigg wiped his mouth with a napkin before responding. "Not bad at all."

Amelia bumped her leg against his, and he bumped hers back. She wanted to laugh and tease him, but she could tell he was trying to keep things nonchalant on this double date. Maybe he'd learn his lesson and stop jumping into her dates after this.

The waitress reappeared, and after Silvia spent what felt like ten minutes asking about specific dishes, she ordered. To the relief of everyone. Grigg gave a slight shake of his head, then snapped his menu closed and said, "I'll have the same thing."

Hayden finished off every last oyster, with Silvia gamely trying one more. After the oysters were cleared from the table, Grigg visibly relaxed.

Silvia had apparently struck a chord with Hayden, and he was telling her all about one of his articles, the very same thing he'd told Amelia before everyone arrived.

"I'm just glad the professor didn't order the snails," Grigg said under his breath.

Amelia looked at him out of the corner of her eye. "You mean escargot."

"Whatever," he said. "I mean seriously, the oysters just tasted like the cocktail sauce I put on it, but is that what you want to kiss?"

She blinked. "What are you talking about?" she whispered.

Grigg leaned closer so that their shoulders brushed. Even through her clothing she felt the warmth of his arm. "You know, your goodnight kiss with Hayden."

Amelia did scoff then.

Silvia and Hayden both looked at her. Amelia covered her mouth and made a small coughing sound, then took a drink of her water. "Sorry, continue."

"There's still debate on exactly what started World War I," Hayden continued. "If it hadn't been the assassination of the archduke of Austria and his pregnant wife, then would it have been something else?"

Silvia was apparently a history buff, because she leaned her chin on her hand and was listening intently.

"Who says I'm going to kiss Hayden?" Amelia whispered to Grigg. "It's our first date, and I'm not that kind of girl."

It was his turn to fight his scoff. In fact, his face reddened with the effort of holding back his reaction.

Amelia elbowed him. "Mind your manners, Mr. Edison. I'm technically your boss."

He took a deep, steadying breath. "I know," he whispered. "You won't let me forget it. But you also must face the truth. I've known you for two years, and we've had many a talk about the people we are dating. And you have confessed to me, multiple times, that you *do* kiss on the first date. If it's warranted, of course."

Amelia wanted to laugh. Instead, she bumped her leg against his. "Keep your annoying memories to yourself."

He bumped her back. "I was asking an innocent question. You know, friend to friend."

She stole a glance at him. He was still rather close to her, and an outside observer would say that he was focused on Hayden's war talk, but Amelia knew Grigg was focused on her one hundred percent.

"I'm not going to kiss Hayden tonight," she whispered. "Happy?"

Grigg's smile was slow, causing a fluttering in her belly. "I am, in fact. Surprisingly happy."

6

Grigg was gratified to see Hayden leave them all after the restaurant, saying that he had his car parked down the street.

That left Grigg to walk the two women to their cars. Silvia had driven and met Grigg in front of the restaurant. He'd walked the few blocks from the office, and it seemed that Amelia had walked as well.

She said good night to the both of them, and before Grigg could ask her where her car was, Silvia grasped his hand and tugged him into a hug.

All right then. He gave her a quick hug, then stepped away.

"What are your plans tonight?" Silvia asked with a broad smile.

"Uh, got an early morning tomorrow." He shrugged. "Boring, I know."

She did a slow scan of his person. "Do you like dessert?"

He wasn't sure where she was going with this question. "Yeah. I'm stuffed, though."

With a laugh, Silvia said, "There's always room for dessert."

Again, he didn't know what she was trying to say. "Yeah, but not tonight. I need to get going."

She gave a good-natured shrug. "Suit yourself."

And finally, she opened her car door and climbed in. When she was heading out of the parking lot, Grigg turned to see how far Amelia had gotten. He didn't see her at first, and then he noticed a woman about halfway down the block, walking in heels. Amelia.

"Mills," he said, jogging to catch up with her.

She slowed her steps and turned. Folding her arms, she waited for him, a smile on her face.

"Did you walk too?" she asked.

"I did." He caught up with her, and they began to walk together. "Aren't your feet killing you?"

She lifted her shoulders. "They've had better nights."

Grigg shook his head. "Women."

Amelia smirked. "So . . . how was it with Silvia? She couldn't take her eyes off you."

He chuckled. "Uh, you mean Hayden. I thought she was going to sign up to be his research assistant or something."

"I don't know," she said. "I mean, yeah, she was listening to Hayden's stories, but only to be polite. Didn't you see how she kept inching toward you all night?"

He swallowed. He had noticed that. And then the odd things she'd said at her car. He'd thought things between them were completely platonic—at least on his end. He hoped she didn't think otherwise. There was no way he'd take her out again. Once was plenty.

"I thought you said that things were casual with Silvia," she pressed.

"Oh, they are," Grigg confirmed. "She was too . . . too much of everything. Didn't you notice how I kept somehow moving closer to *you*?"

Amelia might have blushed, but it was hard to tell beneath the streetlamps. "I did notice," she said, her tone light. "That's why I kept elbowing you—to give me some space."

"Really? I thought you wanted to snuggle." He draped an arm over her shoulders and squeezed. He let go quickly so that it was more of a side hug than anything.

Amelia laughed. "Ha. Ha. You were breaking Silvia's heart."

"I don't think she was all that into me," Grigg said. "I mean, she definitely liked checking me out, but Hayden's the real man in her eyes."

"Stop," Amelia said, fake punching his side.

Grigg pretended to double over in pain. Amelia kept laughing.

When she finally sobered and they were back to walking again, she said, "I don't know about Hayden. Things didn't exactly click, but I feel like I should give him another chance."

"You mean another date or another *chance* chance?"

"Another date," she said. "One date isn't really a full indicator to determine if you're compatible with someone else."

Grigg shoved his hands in his pockets. "I think you're right in most cases. But I don't think in Hayden's. He's not the man for you, but I'll let you figure that out on your own. My lips are sealed."

"Oh, thanks, Mr. Relationship Expert," Amelia said with a shake of her head. "I'm starting to regret letting you come on the dates with me."

"Why?" Grigg said, turning so that he was walking backwards with Amelia still walking forward.

"Well, I thought that you'd be more like an older brother on the dates," she said. "You know, less . . . opinionated."

"Believe me, if you did have a brother, he'd be a lot more opinionated than me about who you dated."

Amelia raised her brows, her eyes filling with amusement. "I guess we'll never know."

"I guess not." They reached a street corner and stopped for the traffic light. Grigg turned to face the road. "So are you going to call him tonight? Tomorrow?"

"Nope," Amelia said. "He'll call me."

Grigg bumped her shoulder. "You sound confident."

"I am kind of irresistible," she teased. "You said so yourself."

The light changed, and they started across the street.

Another man walked toward them, going the opposite direction. His shabby clothing and swayed walking told Grigg that not only was he probably homeless but he was also on something.

Grigg grasped Amelia's hand and pulled her closer to him, out of the way of the homeless guy. She moved easily to Grigg's side, her fingers tightening around his. They reached the other curb, and to his absolute surprise, Amelia didn't let go of his hand. So he didn't let go of hers either.

They walked the remainder of the way to the office hand in hand.

It wasn't something Grigg should be overthinking, but he totally was, because Amelia Ambrose was holding his hand. In public. After a double date. And it was really nice.

When they reached the parking garage of the building, Grigg found himself dreading releasing her hand when they got to her car. But it couldn't be helped.

"Where are you parked?" she asked as their steps slowed.

He pointed to the far side of the parking garage. "You know me, always get the worst spot."

She smiled, and in that moment, with her standing by her car, their hands still linked, it would have been so easy. To kiss her. To change everything that they were and had been to each other. He was beyond tempted, but he also wanted to be sure.

"Well, thanks for inviting me to dinner," he said, squeezing her hand.

That seemed to remind her that they were holding hands in the first place. She squeezed back, then released his hand.

Dang.

"You're welcome," she said. "And thanks for entertaining me all night. I know you hated your dinner."

"I don't like to eat what I can't pronounce."

Amelia only laughed. "You and your menu choices, always getting the same thing wherever you go."

Grigg slipped his hands into his pockets for good measure, despite what his heart wanted him to do. "I guess I like the tried and true, the familiar. Not a big fan of changes."

Amelia kept smiling, then moved to her car, where she unlocked it. "Good night, Grigg."

"Good night, Mills."

He waited until she got into her car and pulled out of the parking garage. Then he began the trek to his car. Whistling as he went.

As he drove back to his condo, he listened to the messages that had come in while he'd been at dinner.

His friend Spencer had called. "We're going biking this weekend, bro. You up for it? Jay's coming too."

Grigg smiled. He'd been friends with Jay and Spencer since

moving to Colorado. He'd hooked up with them on the bike trails, and they'd been hanging out ever since. Spencer was a high school football coach, and Jay ran a small dental practice. Both good guys.

The second message was from Silvia. Strange that she'd called and left a message. Maybe something had happened to her car on her drive home? He frowned when he listened to the message. Nothing was the matter with her car, but this was worse.

"Hi, Grigg." Silvia's smooth tone came on. "I'm at your place, and you're not answering your door. Don't tell me you took a detour." A soft laugh. "It's all right, sweetie, I can be patient. And whatever dessert you're getting, order two of them."

Grigg deleted the message. *Please, please, don't be there,* he thought. Maybe he could drive around for a while and hope that she'd give up. But that was ridiculous. If Silvia was really expecting something to happen tonight between the two of them, then obviously he'd somehow led her on. And he had to set her straight. Either in person or on the phone.

If she wasn't at his place by the time he arrived, he'd call her. There was no reason for any of this misconception to go on for even a short time. When he pulled into his complex, sure enough, Silvia was leaning against his front door, scrolling through her phone.

Should it bother him that she knew his address? Of course she had access to everyone's contact information in the building, but wasn't this some sort of breach of privacy?

Grigg exhaled, then turned off his SUV and climbed out. He shoved his hands into his pockets as he walked toward Silvia.

"You're late," she said in a soft voice as he reached the door.

He stopped in front of her, hands still in his pockets. "I wasn't kidding when I said I had an early morning. I hope you had a great time at dinner, but I've really got to get some shut-eye."

She pushed her lips into a pout. "I'm sleepy too, so I thought we could kill two birds with one stone."

Grigg wasn't going to ask her to clarify, because he was pretty sure what she was implying.

"Look, Silvia," he said in a deliberate tone. "You're a great person and a beautiful woman, and well, tonight was nice. But I'm not, um, interested in seeing you outside of work beyond tonight. My life is crazy right now, and I'm not in a place to date regularly or anything."

"Oh, I get it," she crooned. "I totally do."

But her actions spoke otherwise, because she stepped close and ran a hand up his chest. Grigg didn't move. Mostly he was stunned. Silvia continued her path up his chest, then over his shoulder and behind his neck. Pressing herself against him, she kissed him before he could move out of her grasp.

Grigg set his hands on her waist and moved her away. "Silvia—"

She giggled and grasped his shirt with both hands and tugged him toward her again. Before she managed to kiss him a second time, he grasped both her wrists and held her at arm's length from him.

"Please, I'm not kidding."

She yanked out of his grasp, and her eyes flashed in anger. "You're a jerk, you know that?"

He lifted his hands. "I didn't mean to offend you—"

"Shut it." She moved past him, bumping his arm as she went. "Don't call me again. You're officially x'd."

He wasn't sure what she meant, but that was nothing new. Silvia stalked to her car, then roared out of the parking lot. Shaking his head, he went into his dark condo. He sank onto the couch, his mind backtracking to everything that had been said between them that evening. He couldn't come up with a time when he'd encouraged her to be that brazen.

Grigg exhaled and rubbed at his temples. Then he grabbed his phone and texted Amelia.

Hope your arrival home was less eventful than mine.

He smiled when his phone rang.

"What happened?" Amelia asked when Grigg answered.

He proceeded to tell her what Silvia had done, and Amelia laughed.

"It's not funny," Grigg insisted. "I mean, it kind of is now, but not at the time. I totally got x'd by her."

Amelia only laughed more. "I told you, and you didn't believe me. You were just using Hayden as a cover, but the truth is now out. Silvia digs you. Well, she did until you broke her shiny little heart."

"Her dress *was* kind of shiny."

They both laughed.

The coldness that he'd felt from Silvia had now completely dissipated into warmth.

7

"Sorry to hear about your grandma," Amelia told Hayden over the phone.

"Thanks," he said. "She's ninety-three, so it's no surprise, but still hard."

"Yeah," Amelia agreed. Her own grandma was getting up there, and Amelia had been a pretty lame granddaughter the past few years. She only went to Ambrose for required family events, and never just to visit her grandma. Not that Lillian Ambrose was exactly someone to spend a peaceful afternoon with. The woman still worked full days and possibly half the night.

"I'll call you when I get back," Hayden assured Amelia. "I'm not sure how it's been a week since our date. You're a busy woman, but I'm sorry to miss the concert tonight."

Over the past week, Hayden had called or texted her every day. Amelia had forgotten how persistent he could be. The last time they were together and had broken up, Hayden had called her for about two weeks straight after she'd told him things were over for good. She hadn't replied to anything. He was a bit of a clingy personality. Well, compared to the other men she'd dated or, er, broken up with. Those other men had gone off the grid right away.

But was that a problem if she was in love with him? Being together a lot was what most couples in love did, right?

"Yes, call me when you get back," she said. "That would be great."

They hung up, and Amelia stared at the opposite wall for a moment. It was times like these that she was grateful for her private office. Hayden had called in the middle of the workday, and Amelia would normally let it go to voicemail. But she'd been excited about the concert she'd invited him to tonight, so she'd answered.

Then she'd found out that he'd be getting on a plane to rush back to his California hometown and help with funeral preparations for his grandma.

So what to do with the two concert tickets? She'd told Grigg that he was off the hook for this particular date. The concert had been sold out for months, but she'd been able to snag two tickets, not four. Maybe she could give them to a couple of others in the office. Except . . . Amelia really wanted to go.

Another phone call came in, but this one Amelia sent to voicemail. Unknown number. She'd see if they left a message. She needed a few moments to do one more review of the accounts payable and receivable of Canon Copy Distribution. Their meeting was scheduled to start in ten minutes, and the phone call with Hayden had eaten up precious time.

Her desk intercom buzzed, and her assistant, Polly, said, "Meeting in five."

"Thanks, Polly." Amelia clicked over to one of the spreadsheets on her screen and double-checked some of the numbers. Some of Canon's equipment was out of date, by about ten years, and upgrading would be expensive at first but save money in the long run. Plus make them more competitive.

A rap sounded on her door, and before she could invite the person in, the door opened.

Of course it was Grigg. Ready for their meeting.

Like an obedient partner, he was wearing a suit, and his white shirt was pristine. Grigg underestimated himself in a suit, and on the days he wore one, he definitely got noticed. Well, he always got noticed. Funny that he seemed oblivious to it most of the time. Amelia had witnessed him turning down offers of phone numbers plenty of times.

Or if he did take a number, he'd delete the number moments later.

"Ready, Mills?" Grigg asked.

"One sec," she said, then clicked on two more columns, scanned the numbers, and looked up. "What did you think about their wholesale price for paper receivables?"

Grigg walked into the office and around her desk so that he could get a look at the open spreadsheet. Placing his hands on the desk, he leaned down.

Amelia tried not to inhale too deeply, but she couldn't avoid the scent of Grigg's subtle spicy cologne this close to him.

"I think they're highballing for some reason," Grigg said. "When we worked with Stanford Printing, their wholesale paper costs weren't nearly so high."

Amelia loved Grigg's head for numbers. "That's what I thought too, but I wasn't sure. Something felt off, though."

"Yeah." Grigg reached across her and placed his hand over the mouse. Then he toggled to the formula at the bottom of the subtotal cell. "Aha."

"What?" Amelia asked.

"They've put in an eighteen percent markup in the subtotal."

"So the numbers in the column aren't a sum of the subtotal?"

"Correct."

Amelia leaned back in her chair as Grigg stepped away and folded his arms.

"What are you thinking?" she asked.

"That someone in their company is skimming money off the top," he said. "Trying to get higher funding from us, when in fact their costs will be well covered by a lower amount."

"What do you want to do?" Amelia asked. "What if it's someone in the meeting? Or the president herself?"

Grigg exhaled. "We lay it all out. Make sure we have our security cameras on in case this goes south. But we need to drop them as clients until things are resolved on their end."

"Right." Amelia stood. She wasn't too happy about losing this client since they'd been family owned for decades. But she also hated that there might be internal corruption.

Grigg hadn't moved back or given her space, so they were standing rather close.

He hadn't shaved for a couple of days, which made Amelia envious that men could get away with going a little rogue and still look sexy. She swallowed. Had she just thought of Grigg as *sexy*?

This whole free-from-the-curse thing was really getting to her. "Well, let's get in there, I guess. The news won't deliver itself."

But Grigg still didn't budge. "Tonight's your second date with Hayden?"

Usually he was teasing her about the dating stuff, but his gaze was serious.

"Actually . . . he just canceled. His grandma passed away."

One of his brows lifted. "Oh, that's too bad." His next question was to be expected. "What are you doing with the concert tickets?"

Amelia rubbed the side of her neck, feeling antsy for some reason. Had she seen hope in Grigg's eyes?

"I don't know yet," she said. "Maybe I'll go alone."

Grigg gave a fake cough. "Oh, look," he said, pulling his phone from his pocket. "My schedule's completely free tonight. I mean, I had like three other obligations, but they were all just canceled." His dark-brown eyes refocused on her. "I'll buy dinner."

So it wasn't that Amelia hadn't considered asking Grigg, in the five minutes since Hayden's cancelation, but a concert? And now dinner? That was a lot of one-on-one time together. Without work to distract her. And she was known to get a little crazy at concerts. Then again, they would be surrounded by thousands of people at the concert. Not really alone. Dinner before would also be surrounded by other people. She could suggest the sports grill a block away from the stadium, and that place was plenty busy and loud.

The intercom came on again. "Ms. Ambrose, the executives of Canon Copy have arrived, and I've put them in the conference room."

"Thanks, Polly, I'm on my way."

"Well?" Grigg said in a quiet voice, although the intercom had clicked off.

She exhaled. "All right."

He grinned, then did the most unexpected thing. Before she could take another breath, he'd pulled her into a tight hug. She didn't even have time to react before he'd released her.

"Wow. It's like I made your day or something."

"Oh, you did." He strode to the office door and opened it. "After you, Mills."

She might have felt a bit unsteady on her feet after that unexpected hug, but she picked up her laptop, straightened her shoulders, and headed out the door. She also might have noticed the way Grigg still smelled nice as she passed by him.

They'd hugged before, right? No big deal. Friends hugged. Co-workers hugged.

Despite her reasoning, her thoughts were distracted during the meeting with Canon Copy, and Grigg ended up doing most of the talking. And even when he broke the bad news of someone in the company doctoring numbers and proceeded to walk the executives through the evidence he'd found, Amelia was still thinking about Grigg's spontaneous hug and their upcoming evening together. Just the two of them. And thousands of concertgoers. Still.

Grigg was a natural presenter, and he spoke in a way that everyone understood. If he sensed someone wasn't quite understanding, he wouldn't call them out on it but would explain in a different way. At one point, he adjusted his tie, and Amelia's gaze went to his tanned throat. That got her thinking about what he'd done on the weekends, or evenings, to get that tan of his. He was a fit man. Not made of muscle like Bryce, but Amelia found that she appreciated general fitness versus someone whose every spare moment was taken up with exercise and nutrition.

They'd never talked about sports or exercising or what Grigg might do to stay in shape. What he could do since his knee injury. After hearing his tale of woe soon after they began working together, she hadn't talked to him about football. It sort of felt like an off-the-table topic.

And . . . here she was, *checking out Grigg*. Practically ogling him. What was wrong with her?

The meeting went over schedule by an hour, not surprisingly with the twist of events, and by the time the last Canon Copy employee had left, Amelia needed a break. From the office, from the spreadsheets, from her thoughts of Grigg.

"How do you think it went?" Grigg said when it was just the two of them left in the conference room.

"Better than I thought," Amelia said. "Do you think it was one of the executives?"

"I do," Grigg said in a solemn tone. "Probably the CFO. He's the closest to the numbers, and if he's worth his salt he would have caught something earlier."

"Which means he's the guilty party."

"Correct." Grigg's mouth lifted into a smile. "You were kind of distracted. Thinking about the concert?"

"Uh, yeah," she said, giving a fleeting smile in return. "I need to run a quick errand. Can you tell Polly that I'll be back in an hour?"

Grigg frowned because this was an unusual request and they both knew it.

But Amelia didn't want to get into any explanations right now. So she made her escape and found herself walking to the bookshop on the corner. There, she could lose herself in the aisles and not have to interact with anyone. There, she could analyze why she was being so drawn to Grigg.

8

GRIGG DECIDED HE was going to roll with whatever Amelia wanted to do tonight. In the funding meeting with Canon Copy, she'd been so quiet that he'd wondered if she was sick. And when she came back from whatever her errand had been, she stayed in her office with the door closed. It was after five when Grigg finally knocked on her office door and asked what time and where she wanted to go for dinner.

He cracked open the door to find Amelia not working on her computer, which was unusual. In fact, she was staring into space, at nothing. "Hey," he said. "Is . . . everything okay?"

She snapped her gaze to his. Her blue eyes widened, and she literally blushed.

Well, this was new. What had she been thinking about? Something that made her embarrassed to be caught daydreaming? Hayden? Grigg slipped his hands into his pockets. "I was wondering if I could pick you up for the concert?"

The blush hadn't left her cheeks. "No, I thought we could meet at the sports grill." She rose from her desk and began packing up her laptop. "I need to get home and change first, and I don't want you to have to worry about driving in the opposite direction to take me back home after the concert."

Grigg knew it wouldn't do any good to argue with her. When Amelia made up her mind, it was made up. And by the flush on her cheeks and the determined line of her mouth, he knew her mind had been made up. Well, like he had already decided, tonight he was going to go with the flow.

Grigg made it home in record time; apparently the traffic light gods were on his side. His dog, Boomer, was only too happy to see him a little early. The black lab was getting on in years, but he was still never shy about showing his love and appreciation.

"Hey buddy," Grigg said, bending to scratch Boomer's head. The dog wagged his entire body, not just his tail. "You hungry, boy?" It was a stupid question, and both dog and owner knew it. Boomer was always hungry.

"Let's get you fed then, come on," Grigg said, leading the way into the kitchen. He pulled the fridge door open, which meant that Boomer gave an excited bark. "Yep, that's right. You're getting a treat tonight, because I have a date with a beautiful woman."

Grigg watched Boomer eat the couple of hot dogs he'd put into the food bowl. He knew that tonight was not really a date. At least not according to Amelia—and it shouldn't be according to him either. But it was kind of fun to think that if they did end up dating for real someday, then tonight could be considered their first date, in a retrospective sort of way.

While Boomer happily ate his dog food, Grigg headed into the bedroom, where he changed into jeans and a black T-shirt, which was probably standard wear for concerts everywhere. His knee was already bothering him more than usual this week, so he was sure to slip on a light knee brace underneath his pants. Usually he wore it when he went running or worked out. Although his running days were going to be coming to an end soon. So biking was his exercise of choice, which might eventually change to swimming laps at the rec pool. Or at least that was what his doctors had warned him about.

But his true passion outside of work was fixing up a small cabin in the Morrison area. He'd bought the property soon after starting with the firm, and most of his weekends he spent at the cabin making repairs. Someday it would be livable, but unless he hired a construction crew, that day was far off.

As luck would have it, he was early to the sports grill. The traffic lights were still cooperating, even with the extra congestion from concertgoers. It was probably a good thing he was sitting at the bar drinking some ice water when Amelia walked in. He'd assumed she would wear something casual, like jeans and a T-shirt, similar to his outfit. But instead of casual wear or her usual business suit, she was wearing a pale-pink summer dress. The sleeves were strappy and the bodice fitted, and the skirt danced about her knees as she walked toward him. She wasn't exactly wearing high heels, but her sandals were high enough that he wondered if she planned on sitting through the whole concert. Because at every concert he had been to lately, no one had sat down.

He supposed he was still checking her out when she noticed him, which meant that he was caught ogling her. *I might as well own up to it.* She wore a barely there smile as she continued walking toward him. He stood and greeted her with the truth. "You look beautiful, Mills."

She merely smiled. "Don't think I dressed up for you, cuz." She grasped the edges of her skirt and looked down. "This was already planned for tonight."

Grigg placed a hand over his heart. "Oh, I didn't think you had dressed up for little old me. I mean, you always look beautiful. But I must say, I do like you in that dress." This time she *did* blush.

"Come on," he said, "our table's ready." He took her hand, because the restaurant was crowded and she didn't know where they were going. So he might as well lead her. He didn't look at her as he led her through the maze of tables, but he sensed her surprise at his action. Her hand was cool in his, and although he didn't link their fingers, there was plenty of warmth between their palms.

Grigg pulled out the chair at their table for two, then signaled the waitress. She was over in a flash and took their drink orders, then left them to peruse the menu.

"Wow, Grigg," Amelia told him. "That was special treatment."

He shrugged. "I've been here a time or two."

Amelia's brows raised, so he decided to clarify. "Not on *dates*—well, not all the time." He smiled, because in truth he was having fun with this. "I'm not much of a cook, so I eat out a lot."

"You don't like to cook, or you refuse to cook?"

"Both, I guess." Grigg didn't need to look at his menu, because he already knew what he was ordering. No surprise there. "What about you? Do you like to cook?"

"I gave up on that a long time ago," she said with a laugh. "Me and hot pans and burning ovens don't really get along too well."

"Sounds like there's a story in that," he said.

"I just don't get how the beautiful recipes on Pinterest never turn out like the picture."

"You know, they probably get those recipe pictures from Google Images or something," he said. "Also there are food stylists and photographers."

"Yeah, you're right." She picked up her menu. "What are you ordering? Do you have a regular dish here?"

"I have two regular dishes here," he said with a wink. "It's either the salmon or the braised chicken."

"The salmon sounds good."

"I would highly recommend it, Mills." Griggs liked her in pink summer dresses. He liked it very much. He wondered if he'd ever seen her wear that color before. But to bring attention again to her looks or to mention how beautiful she was might be going a bit overboard. "So what's the next step with Hayden? After his grandma's funeral, of course."

She shrugged. "He said he'd call me when he gets back in town, no real plans yet."

"No future concerts on the horizon?"

"Nope, this was the plan I had," she said.

"One point for me I guess," Grigg sad.

Amelia smirked. "It's not a contest, Grigg. You're not even on the list."

Should he go for it? "What are the requirements to get on the list? I mean, I'm asking for a friend, of course, a special friend who might be interested in being on that list." He wasn't sure how she would react, and perhaps he shouldn't have even said anything. Because this could get awkward fast.

Thankfully she laughed, her blue eyes gleaming. "Well, you can tell your *friend* that the list is closed. If number five doesn't work out, then I'm going back to my usual routine."

"Ouch." Grigg shook his head. "You're one tough woman, Mills. You won't even give my friend a chance?"

Amelia gazed at him for a minute, and Grigg gazed right back. She could read into this any way she wanted. But maybe it was time for him to stick a toe in the water. Just to see how warm the temperature was.

"What are you doing, Grigg?"

"About ready to order dinner," he said.

She tilted her head. "Just don't get any ideas, big guy. You know we're total opposites."

Had she really said that? Had she really opened the gates to talk of a relationship between them? Well, he supposed he had unlocked them. Just then, the waitress returned. Grigg ordered the salmon, and Amelia did too. He felt pretty triumphant that she ordered the same meal, because he was going to totally use it against her.

"We're not so opposite after all," he said. "We both ordered salmon."

Amelia took a slow drink of the water that the waitress had brought as well. "Are we really going to talk about this right now?"

"It's up to you," he said. "We can talk after the concert. Maybe we could go get dessert somewhere? Or we can meet for coffee in the morning? I know a great café."

"Does a woman named Maggie work there?"

Grigg laughed. "Touché."

Their conversation steered to other topics, which consisted mostly of work. Grigg noticed that the more they talked about work and not about personal stuff, the more relaxed Amelia became. Soon it was time to leave for the concert, and as they walked toward the stadium, Amelia kept up a running chatter about one of their long-term clients and some of the changes that they wanted to make within the company. Grigg agreed with all of her suggestions, and he held back from changing the topic, even though he still wanted to talk about how his *friend* could get on her list.

Although they had reserved seats, the people surrounding them had no concept of personal space. And a time or two they were jostled until they ended up being forced to stand pretty close together, which of course Grigg didn't mind in the least. He could tell Amelia was making a valiant effort to keep at least a couple inches of space between their bodies. But when her favorite song came on, it was apparently everyone else's favorite as well, and all personal space requirements were thrown out the window.

Everyone was dancing, including Amelia. Grigg tried to give her some dancing room, but he also had a laugh. He had never seen Amelia so caught up in a moment that she forgot her natural reserves. When she caught him grinning at her, she smiled and grabbed his hand. A very surprising move on her part, and very welcome on his part.

When the next song came on, it was significantly slower. Grigg was only too pleased when she kept hold of his hand. In fact, a couple more teenagers crowded into their aisle, apparently best friends with whoever else had reserved seats in their section, which only pushed Grigg and Amelia closer together.

So it was only natural to stand behind Amelia and to rest his hands lightly on her waist, if only to keep the both of them from being jostled by the other singing, screaming, and jumping new friends of theirs.

Amelia didn't pull away or try to move out of Grigg's hold. She continued to sway with the music, and he swayed with her.

Teens bumped into them multiple times, laughing, dancing, not caring who they touched. Grigg tightened his hold on Amelia, and she leaned back until she was securely in his arms.

Her scent was soft and sweet, reminding him of strawberries. The music, the dim lighting, and the feel of her in his arms was an ambrosia.

"Put me on your list," he whispered in her ear.

He didn't think she'd heard him, because she didn't respond. She merely kept dancing, and he kept swaying with her. When the final song was over and the band started an encore, he said, "Do you want to beat the crowds out of here?"

She turned then, her body still pressed against his. "They always do two encores."

"So you want to stay?"

She nodded.

"All right." This wasn't so bad, he told himself as she turned and leaned against him again.

He slipped his arms around her waist, and she didn't seem to mind. She was right. There was a second encore, and no one left the stadium. Not even after the band left and the regular lights came on. Everyone was still calling out for a third encore.

"This is crazy," Grigg said.

"Let's go," she said suddenly, drawing away from him. The absence of her body against his felt like someone had doused him with cold water. She snatched his hand and drew him out of their section. The stadium aisles were starting to fill up, and the going was slow.

The crowd was still chanting for the band to return, and Grigg had to admire their fortitude. The stairway had become so crowded that it was impossible to go up or down.

"Here," Grigg said, "I'll go in front of you and pave the way."

He barely heard Amelia's reply, but it seemed to be in the affirmative. So he pushed his way through the crowd, bringing Amelia with him. They'd finally reached the main level of the stadium when the crowd erupted into a deafening roar. Grigg snapped his head around. The band had returned for a third encore.

Amelia grasped his arm. "They're back!"

They stopped where they were and watched. Everything was in place—the music, the lights, the special effects—and Grigg had no doubt this had been planned. And the fans were eating it up.

Amelia kept her grasp on his arm, and when others jostled against them, he wrapped his arm about her shoulder so they wouldn't get separated. She slipped both arms about his waist, and Grigg didn't mind at all, even if it was just to hold on.

9

AMELIA WAS WALKING on hot coals, not just because her feet ached but because her pulse wouldn't stop racing. And it wasn't because of the amazing concert she and Grigg had just watched.

They'd touched a lot tonight: they'd held hands and leaned into each other, and his arms had been around her waist during the last part of the concert. She'd felt both exhilarated and nervous, yet she hadn't pulled away from him.

Now they walked toward the parking lot where both of them had left their cars. Amelia folded her arms against the chill of the night, and Grigg walked with his hands in his pockets. The silence between them was like a breathing thing after the loud noise of the concert. All night he'd been dropping hints about being on her list. He'd gone so far as to *ask* to be put on her list, and she'd pretended not to hear him. But she knew she wasn't fooling him. He knew she'd heard.

"Where are you parked?" Grigg asked.

"Third row," she said. "You don't need to walk me there. Tons of people are around, you know."

He cast her a sideways glance that said she must be kidding.

So they kept walking. She didn't need to point out her car once they reached the third row, since the bright-red color gleamed beneath the parking lot lights.

With every step that brought her closer to her car, she felt like time was slipping through her fingers, time in which she needed to explain herself to Grigg. In more than one subtle way, he'd let her know he was interested. In her.

She still couldn't wrap her mind around it. His dating stories had never led her to believe she was his type anyway. He always went out with women who were outdoorsy or hipster-ish. And if she and Grigg dated, then . . . well, it would change everything.

When they reached her car, she pulled out her key fob, then turned to face him at last. "Look, Grigg, I don't know exactly how to say this, but—"

He stepped close to her and placed a hand on her shoulder. His dark eyes bore into hers, more serious than she'd ever seen them. "Then don't say it, Mills," he said in a quiet voice. "Until you know what you really want to say, don't say anything."

She bit the edge of her lip. "That's not fair."

He scanned her face, and it was like she felt the heat of his gaze all the way to her stomach. Who was this man, and what had he done with her easygoing business partner?

"I think it's absolutely fair," he said. "I might be preventing you from making a huge mistake."

She wanted to ask him what he meant, exactly, but his thumb brushed the top of her shoulder. Against her bare skin, his fingers were simply warm, but below her skin, she was heating up. Her pulse was acting like she'd sprinted to the car instead of leisurely strolling.

"Grigg, I think—" This time she cut herself off. His fingers were totally distracting her. She should move his hand. Or tell him to do it. But she did neither.

"*What* do you think, babe?"

Her breath caught. "I think you shouldn't be calling me *babe*. I'm your business partner."

He blinked as if he'd been in some sort of fog. "You're right. I'll stop calling you babe if you add me to your list."

She stared at him. Had he really said that? Grigg Edison? Slowly, she released her breath.

"You don't have to answer now," he said, that hand still on her shoulder, making her legs feel like water. "Think about it. Take your time."

"Grigg..." Her voice trailed off, because in his eyes she saw desire. And she was pretty sure he saw the same thing in her eyes. And it was true, she realized. Right now, right here, she desired Grigg Edison. Tomorrow morning she'd regret everything about tonight, but right now, she wanted to pull him close. Breathe him in. Find out what it was like to kiss him.

Instead, she reached for his hand and firmly removed it from her shoulder.

He merely nodded, then stepped away. Sliding his hands in his pockets, he said, "Good night, Amelia. Thanks for the invite."

Her words had all fled, and she didn't know when they'd return.

She said nothing as she watched him walk away. When he disappeared in a crowd of concertgoers looking for their cars, Amelia finally slid into the driver's seat of her car. But she didn't pull out and get into the long line of traffic exiting the parking lot. Instead, she leaned her head back and closed her eyes. Grigg wanted to be on her list. And she was almost positive that if she had allowed it, he would have taken things to the next level tonight. Maybe asked her out? Maybe kissed her?

She didn't know, but now that the topic had been opened between them, she knew they could never go back to what they were before. Which made her sad, because she knew she couldn't date Grigg. They were co-workers, and what would happen if things went south?

Their work environment would be more than strained. Although ... how would it be now? Amelia blew out a breath of frustration, knowing that this would be a long weekend, waiting for Monday morning to see how everything was going to play out between them.

She should call him right now and tell him no way. Then be done with it.

But a small part of her didn't want to turn him down so harshly and directly. So what did that mean? That she *was* interested?

In cases like this, she'd usually call a friend and get advice, but Grigg was her friend.

It wasn't like she could call her mom—a woman who'd been married multiple times—besides, they rarely talked.

She couldn't call Sofia, her oldest half sister, because they'd never been close like that. Maybe Lauren . . . they weren't that close either, but she was the type Grigg usually went after, so maybe she'd know *his* type. If that made sense.

Good thing California time was behind Denver, so while still sitting in the parking lot, Amelia called Lauren.

She answered on the second ring.

"Hey, Lauren," Amelia said.

"Is everything okay?" Lauren asked immediately.

Did Amelia mention that they weren't all that close, which meant they usually only spoke for emergencies?

"Everything's fine," Amelia said. "I hope it's not too late to call you."

"I seem to be heading into an all-night painting binge."

Lauren was an artist gaining some renown, and Amelia had one of her paintings hanging in her house.

"Well, this should only take a minute," Amelia said. She explained about the list she'd made, and Lauren laughed.

"You're so organized," Lauren said. "A list? Why am I not surprised? How many have you checked off?"

"Two so far," Amelia said. "But that's beside the point. Remember my business partner, Grigg Edison? He started with the firm a couple of years ago."

"Yeah, you've mentioned him."

"Did I also mention that he's single and, uh, good-looking and charming and—" She cut herself off.

Lauren gave a soft laugh. "You didn't mention that, but I'm assuming you've hit a small snag."

"It's bigger than small," Amelia said with a sigh.

"Send me a picture."

"What?" Amelia asked. This was the last thing she'd expected her sister to ask.

"In fact," Lauren said, "send me a picture of all the guys on your list, including Grigg. I'm a visual person, and I'll be able to give you my feedback with more accuracy."

"Okay, hang on a minute." Amelia browsed Facebook and Instagram, then sent screenshots of the three men left on her list. From her photo app, she found one of Grigg from their March Madness office party a few months ago.

"Hmm," Lauren said. "You definitely like men with dark hair."

Amelia scrolled through the pictures herself. Clint was the only blond, but he was off the list and not included in what she'd sent to Lauren.

"I guess I have a type?"

"Dark-haired, athletic type, it seems," Lauren mused. "All right. I've already voted, but I should probably let you figure it out on your own."

"That's not fair," Amelia said. "I called you for advice, and now you refuse to give it?"

Lauren chuckled. "Don't take this the wrong way, but you're kind of a stubborn person, Millie, and if I tell you what I think, you might run the other way. Then you'll go through a bunch of heartache when you realize the mistakes you've made."

"You're really not going to tell me?" Amelia asked. "What if you give me feedback on each of them? General insights? Nothing too persuasive."

"I'm afraid I can't do that either," Lauren said, "because only one of these guys has the extra something."

When Amelia hung up with Lauren, who'd been no help at all, Amelia decided that she'd just proceed with her list. Put Grigg out of her mind, at least for the rest of the weekend, and on Monday she'd break the news to him.

She headed out of the nearly empty parking lot, and when she got home, she might have spent an inordinate amount of time on social media, looking up each of the men on her list. As well as a few things about Grigg.

He biked, apparently. How did she not know that?

And he golfed. Well, that she knew. He'd gone golfing with clients before.

His mom's birthday had been last week.

Amelia sighed and turned off her phone. She'd never get to sleep going down rabbit holes.

By Saturday afternoon, Amelia had given up on being stoic. She had to talk to Grigg. Today. As usual, she'd gone to the office for a couple of hours, so the place was quiet, and she had no excuses not to call him.

Besides, this would all be easier over the phone. But when she finally mustered up the determination to call him, his voicemail clicked on.

Amelia hung up without leaving a message.

Was his phone off? Or had he sent her call to voicemail? Now she couldn't remember if it had rung or gone straight to voicemail. Would he see the missed call on his phone? Should she text him?

Amelia rose from her desk and paced her office. Grigg wasn't on her list, and he was already creating havoc.

Just then, her phone rang, and her heart skipped a couple of beats. Grigg was calling her back, and this made her inordinately glad.

She reached for her phone only to see it was Hayden.

Pushing back the disappointment, she answered. "Hi," she said in a perfectly normal voice. "How's everything going?"

"Fine, considering the circumstances," Hayden said. "I had a few minutes to escape the chaos, so I thought I'd check in with you."

Amelia perched on the edge of her desk. "I should be checking in with *you*," she said.

Hayden chuckled. "You're sweet. And I love that you've been thinking of me. Did you miss me last night?"

It took Amelia a moment to process what he was saying. Oh, yes. The concert. Where she'd been decidedly *not* thinking about him. Grigg had made that quite impossible. "We'll have to go to another concert soon," she said, avoiding answering the question directly.

"That would be amazing." He lowered his voice. "I'm thinking of taking you hiking when I get back on Tuesday. Maybe a picnic? We could leave around four. The hike is only about two hours up, so we could be back down the trail by sunset."

"Tuesday?" Amelia asked, the panic setting in. She couldn't leave work that early. Ever. She didn't even need to check her schedule. Also, Hayden was a bit of a germaphobe. They'd gone hiking once when they'd been dating and he had brought along hand sanitizer, plus cleansing wipes. "Maybe we should save something like a hike for the weekend, when I have more time."

"Right . . ." Hayden gave a rather big sigh. "What should we do on Tuesday, then?"

This, Amelia could work with. "I'll be finished around six thirty, so we could meet for dinner and catch up."

Hayden agreed, then he proceeded to tell her about the dynamics of the family members who'd started to gather for the funeral. Amelia listened, but after about ten minutes of him talking, her attention began to stray. She really did want to get a few things caught up while she was at the office. Besides, she didn't feel like she could really relax and enjoy talking to Hayden while she was so worried over Grigg and what was, or was not, happening there.

"You should have seen her face," Hayden was saying. "You'd think my aunt was about to kick everyone out. Uncle Johnny sure got a laugh . . ."

Amelia wasn't quite sure what Hayden was talking about, so she offered a light laugh. Before the conversation took another ten minutes, she said, "Look, I've got some things to finish up before it gets too late."

"Oh, like what?"

Well, this took her off guard. "I'm working on a financial plan, then I hope to grocery shop today. You know, put some food in my fridge."

"Always working, Amelia," Hayden mused. "I'm assuming you make a pretty good income. Maybe you can use one of those apps to deliver food. Then you'll never have to shut down your laptop."

Amelia stilled. Had she just been insulted?

Then Hayden laughed. "Kidding. You're the best. You know that? Can't wait to see you Tuesday."

After hanging up with him, she pulled up Facebook on her phone and typed in Peter's name. His most recent picture, posted a couple of hours ago, showed him cozy with another woman. And it wasn't his sister. Hmm . . . Now she wasn't too sure if she wanted another repeat of her phone call with Bryce.

So she browsed onto Jack's page. He looked the same. Shaggy, brown hair, blue eyes, a lazy grin. Trust fund guy who was rather brilliant at the same time. Maybe she'd send him a note on Messenger.

10

Grigg weighed the pros and cons of calling Amelia back this weekend as he strapped his bike helmet on after a short break. Two of his buddies had already gone ahead, taking the trail that wound down the mountain side.

When he did a quick check of his phone, he discovered a missed call from Amelia. She hadn't left a message, and she hadn't texted. This pretty much told him she was calling him to answer his question about being put on her list.

So did Grigg want to be turned down today? Or wait until Monday?

Whatever happened, he'd changed his mind. He didn't want to be added to her list. No, he wanted her to rip it up and throw it away. Or burn it. Either would suffice. He didn't want to be a name to be checked off.

He needed a new strategy.

He wouldn't call her back, because that was what the old Grigg would do. The Grigg whom Amelia was indecisive about. He needed to show her he was serious about *them*. And that whatever yahoos she was planning on dating next should be given some competition.

It wasn't something he'd be discussing with his friends, though; he'd talked about Amelia plenty, and they'd never let him live down his crush on her. He took a final swig from his water bottle, then hopped onto his mountain bike. Heading down the trail, he appreciated the early fall day and the chance to enjoy the outdoors. It always seemed to clear his head and center his thoughts.

Which, of course, circled back to Amelia.

"Hey slowpoke," Jay called out as Grigg rounded the final bend of the trail that bottomed into the parking lot. "We were about to leave you a note to find your own way back. What were you doing up there?"

Grigg scoffed. He'd been ten minutes behind Jay and Spencer, max.

"Sorry for the inconvenience," he chimed. He made quick work of breaking down his bike and loading it into the back of the SUV he'd driven. Then he settled into the driver's seat and turned the AC on full blast.

Jay leaned forward from the back seat. "Spencer's barbecuing tonight. Want to come?"

"Yeah, I already picked up the steaks," Spencer said. "Melanie's going to be there."

"Uh, no," Grigg said. Keeping away from Melanie was a priority.

"She's not going to pounce on you," Spencer said with a laugh. "She's, um . . . interested in someone else."

Grigg's gaze connected with Jay's in the rearview mirror. "Are you serious, dude? You and Melanie?"

His friend's stained cheeks were the answer. "I was going to tell you, but there wasn't really an opportunity."

"A four-hour bike ride in Mother Nature with nothing but the birds to interrupt wasn't enough of an opportunity?" Grigg said.

Spencer laughed. Jay scowled.

"I didn't want things to be awkward," Jay said.

Grigg shrugged. "We were never serious, and I'm definitely not interested in reconciling. So as far as I'm concerned, you can date Melanie free and clear."

A smile spread across Jay's face.

"Maybe I will come." Grigg's mind churned with ideas, lots of them. "Not to see Melanie again—I'll leave her to you, Jay." He'd invite Amelia. She knew these friends of his, and it would give him more of a reason to call her back.

When Grigg was back at his place and showered and changed again, he finally called Amelia. Maybe she wouldn't answer, and that would be that, until Monday at least.

"Hey," she answered, and he immediately tried to decipher her tone of voice.

Was it all-business Amelia? Or open-to-ideas Amelia?

"Hey, Mills," he said. "Spencer's having a barbecue with the guys, and a few gals, of course. Want to come tonight?"

He heard the pause in her breath. He knew she was weighing the invitation against whatever work she was planning on doing.

"It's Saturday," he said. "The weekend? You know, when people throw on shorts and maybe hike or play badminton?"

"I don't know about hanging out with a bunch of people, Grigg."

Well, her tone was definitely serious, subdued.

"Tell you what," he said, "I'll pick you up at seven unless you text me beforehand to cancel."

Another pause. "I shouldn't," she said. "I didn't sleep much last night, so I'm sort of a grouch, and I don't know if I want to deal with Jay's twenty questions."

She was right. Jay had been known to ask Amelia a lot of questions. But Grigg suspected it was because Jay had a small crush on her. Now with Melanie in the picture, maybe that meant fewer questions. "Melanie will be there."

"You want moral support or something?" Amelia asked, her tone sounding more normal now.

"Not exactly," he said. "She and Jay are dating."

Amelia made a half laughing, half choking sound. "Serious?"

"Yep, and they both have my blessing," he said. "I'm kind of relieved, actually."

Her voice lowered. "You are?"

"I am." He wanted to add more, maybe flirt a little, but he refrained because he was having a good feeling she might just come to the barbecue with him.

"I'll see you at seven, unless, you know, I don't." He hung up with a smile on his face, and he'd bet she had one too.

It was definitely progress, and she hadn't given him any bad news.

And by the time he pulled into her condo complex at ten minutes before seven, she still hadn't texted him. All good. When he knocked on her door, he still wasn't a hundred percent sure this was all going to happen tonight, but then the door swung open.

Well, she wasn't wearing a pink sundress, but she looked pretty darn cute anyway. Her denim capris were coupled with a pale-yellow T-shirt that hugged her curves. No concealing business suit tonight. Her dark hair was pulled into a high ponytail that only emphasized the smooth curve of her neck.

"Ready, cuz?" he asked, although his scan of her was nothing close to cousin-friendly.

Her blue eyes met his, and in them he saw questions, complications, and possibly curiosity. He'd go with the curiosity for now.

"Who else is going to be there?" she asked.

"You and me," he said. "The rest are just fill-ins."

He loved her laughter, especially now. "We don't have to stay long if you don't want to."

"I'll let you know." She stepped through the doorway and pulled the door shut behind her. When she had locked it, she followed him to his SUV. He opened the door for her, and she climbed in, making this all feel like a date.

Grigg wasn't complaining. As he drove out of her parking lot, she said, "So are we going to talk about last night?"

He glanced over at her. "If you want."

She didn't say anything for a moment, just gazed out the window. "Hayden called. He'll be back Tuesday, and he wanted to go on a four-hour hike, but I talked him into dinner again."

Grigg nodded. "I can meet you with another double date. Anyone but Silvia."

She smirked. "If it's too much of a pain, don't worry about it. My list is getting pretty short anyway. It looks like Peter might have a girlfriend, at least according to his Facebook pictures."

Grigg slowed the SUV at a stoplight. Looking over at her, he said, "So that leaves Jack?"

"Yeah."

"Even if I never make your list, we're still friends, right?"

Her chest rose with a breath as she held his gaze. "Right."

"I think the yellow T-shirt makes your eyes look bluer."

She tilted her head. "I think you're avoiding something."

"What do you mean?"

"Like why don't *you* date more?" she asked. "You can't fool me, Grigg. You go out with a woman once or twice, then you're done. And don't tell me it's because of something that happened years ago in college."

"You're right," he said. "It's not because of college." The light changed, and he pulled forward, then switched lanes.

She folded her arms, and he noticed the rash of goose bumps on her skin. He reached for the AC and turned it down a notch.

"I don't date much because there's not many women who measure up to my favorite woman."

She scoffed. "You can't compare women to your mom."

He burst out with a laugh. Then kept laughing until he had to wipe the tears from his eyes. He should really pull over and compose himself. Amelia grabbed the wheel to help keep him steady.

When he could finally talk and breathe normally, they were nearly to Spencer's place. Spencer had renovated an old brownstone, and the place looked great. Grigg parked behind a sports car and turned off the ignition.

"You're funny, Mills," he said, opening his door.

Amelia was out of her seat before he could walk around the SUV and open her door. He told himself it was okay, not a sign or anything.

"I'm not trying to be funny," she said as they headed up the walkway to the front door. "You just need to be realistic."

He cut his gaze to her. "I am being realistic. The woman I compare other women to isn't my mom. It's you."

Amelia opened her mouth, closed it, and looked away. The flush had returned to her cheeks. Then she stopped in the middle of the walkway and folded her arms. "Why are you changing everything all of a sudden, Grigg? Everything between us has been fine, totally fine, until you decided to . . ." Her gaze searched his, and he wasn't sure how to read her.

"Decided to . . . what?"

She waved a hand toward his person. "You know, ask to be on my list."

He moved closer. To her credit, she didn't back down. "You're the one who's changing everything. Before you heard from your half sisters about the curse being broken, I knew where I fit in your life. But now, if there's a chance, then I'm going to go for it."

Her eyes widened.

"Get rid of the list, Amelia," he said. "So *you* can face reality."

The flush on her face deepened. And he was pretty sure she was about to chew him out, but the front door opened.

"You guys coming in, or are you watching the grass grow?" Jay asked.

Melanie was with him, practically hanging on him.

"We're coming," Grigg said, moving his gaze back to Amelia, as if to ask her again—*are we going to the barbecue?*

"Hi, Jay," Amelia said, turning and smiling.

Inwardly, Grigg sighed with relief. So what if he had just put his heart on the line and set himself up for getting rejected before he could even start dating Amelia?

"Hi, Melanie, nice to see you again," Amelia continued, basically ignoring Grigg.

Which was fine with him. They were here, together, and hopefully that meant they'd leave together. And hopefully that would give Amelia some time to get over her shock.

They stayed longer than Grigg had thought Amelia would be able to stand. Three hours later, he was driving her back home. She'd seemed to have a good time, and for that he was glad. He was always glad when she took a break from work, however small.

She'd been quiet on the drive so far, so he asked, "Do you need help with anything before Monday's meetings?"

"Are you serious?"

"When am I not serious?"

She sighed, but it was a soft sigh. "I'd love a second pair of eyes on the spreadsheet for Richards and Sons Plumbing. I can't get a couple of things to balance."

"Sure, no problem," he said.

She nodded, and when they parked, he decided to take the initiative and walk her to her door.

He waited a moment while she unlocked her door, then he said, "I'll go over it tonight and let you know what I find out."

She looked up at him, her brow furrowed. "I thought you could come inside and look at it with me. I don't think it will take long. Unless you have plans with Jenny."

"Ha." He knew she was teasing. At the barbecue, a woman named Jenny had paid him plenty of attention. He'd been nice, but not too friendly. She'd tried to trade numbers with him, so he finally told her he was dating someone. A white lie he hoped wouldn't be a lie for much longer. "I encouraged Jenny to get to know Spencer better. Hopefully she took my advice."

"You're so generous to your friends," Amelia said, pushing the door open.

Grigg followed. "I'm a nice guy, I guess."

She flipped on lights and continued toward the kitchen area.

Grigg had been inside her place a handful of times, always for work-related reasons, but this somehow felt different. It was hard to explain, but he could feel the tension radiating from her. It wasn't a bad tension; it was . . . more like anticipation. Was she expecting anything from him? Besides his usual declarations of asking to be on her list?

She brought her laptop to the kitchen table.

Grigg always marveled at the way Amelia lived so simply. Knowing that she was worth millions in personal funds only impressed him more because she didn't flaunt her wealth at all. In fact, since he oversaw their firm's books, he knew she was the key investor of the firm itself and that she was generous in her charity contributions.

"Do you want anything to drink?" she asked, moving to the fridge. "Water? Soda?"

"You have soda?"

"Well, no . . ." She shrugged and smiled.

He laughed. "Water's fine. Thanks." He sat at the table and turned the laptop toward him. Scanning through the columns told him two things. The plumbing company's overhead was ridiculously high, and it seemed they had a benefit package that was overpriced as well.

Amelia joined him at the table, and he took a drink of the water, then pointed out what he'd noticed right off the bat.

She rested her chin on her hand. "How do you figure this stuff out so fast? I mean, I've spent hours on this, and you've been here two minutes."

Grigg shifted back in his chair so he could look her in the eyes. "We used to do case studies all the time in college. Nothing is really new anymore, so I guess you could say that I've seen stuff like this before. Makes it easier to notice."

She nodded, her gaze moving over him.

He'd give more than a penny for her thoughts. Maybe a hundred bucks.

"So what do you suggest we tell them?"

"First they need to shop their benefits plan and find another provider," he said. "Then they might be smart to relocate. The neighborhood they're in has become trendy over the past few years, and they could save a lot of overhead if they relocated. Customers find them on the internet anyway, not by a storefront."

Amelia nodded. "Yeah, you're right. All excellent suggestions." She heaved a breath and looked away.

Grigg waited a moment. This contemplative side of Amelia was one he rarely saw. But it gave him the chance to study her profile, the way her hair now tumbled over her shoulders since she'd taken out her ponytail when they walked into the apartment, how she'd kicked off her shoes already.

"What's wrong, Mills?" he asked in a quiet voice.

Without looking at him, she said, "I'm thinking of adding you to my list."

11

AMELIA FROZE. HAD she just spoken aloud? By the silence in the kitchen, she was pretty sure the answer was *yes*. But thinking it and saying it were two completely different things.

She stood, rapidly, and bumped her knee on the table. Which hurt. A lot.

"Um, I'll be right back." Then she left the kitchen and hurried down the hall. Once in her bedroom she stood in the middle of the room in the dark. Trying to breathe.

What had she said? And what was she doing right now? "Real mature," she whispered to herself. No sound came from the kitchen. What was Grigg doing? What was he thinking?

She kept her eyes squeezed shut, willing her rebellious heart to stop pounding so hard. She'd wanted Grigg to kiss her after the concert, and she wanted him to come after her now . . .

She was dating Hayden, right? She should be focusing on him. One man at a time. But a few of the things that Hayden had said were bothering her more and more. And she really didn't mind Grigg interfering. Exhaling slowly, she opened her eyes. She had to get back to the kitchen. Figure out how to get over the nervous jumping in her veins.

"Amelia?" Grigg said, his voice low and coming from the hallway outside her bedroom. "Are you okay?"

No, she wasn't okay. "Hang on. I had to get something." She

turned and walked out of the room and found Grigg leaning against the wall, hands in his pockets.

The light from the kitchen made the hallway dim, but she could see him clearly enough.

"Seems like you want to take me off your list before I technically got added on." His tone was light, teasing.

Her throat was a lump. Why was this so hard? It was only Grigg. "I think I've lost my mind," she said. "I mean, I thought calling these guys would be a good idea, but truthfully, I don't want to see Hayden again."

"So cancel your dinner."

She lifted her chin. "I think I will."

His smile was slow, and he moved toward her. There was nowhere to go in the hallway, so she didn't move.

His hand brushed against hers, and he loosely linked their fingers. "What are you afraid of, babe?"

Biting the edge of her lip, she looked down at their hands. He rubbed his thumb over her fingers, and goose bumps traveled up her arm.

"Everything," she whispered. "I'm afraid that I'll always be cursed, even if my half sisters aren't."

Grigg lifted his other hand and moved his fingers along her jaw. She had to look at him then. His brown eyes were almost black in the dim lighting, but they were plenty warm.

"And I'm afraid that if we date, and if the curse can truly be broken and you don't die—"

"Oh, thank you," Grigg deadpanned.

"—but things still don't work out, that it will hurt too much."

Grigg's hand moved to her neck, his touch soft and warm, his gaze steady on hers. "The last thing I'd ever do is hurt you."

"I know." She breathed in everything that was him. "But losing your friendship would hurt."

Grigg lowered his head and touched his forehead to hers. "You sure know how to deter a guy from making a move."

She smiled. "Sorry."

"I don't want to lose our friendship either," he said in a quiet voice. "But I can't keep pretending that I *only* want to be friends with you. We've worked together for two years, Mills, and that's plenty of time to know that I'm not going to be changing my mind about you."

Being this close to Grigg was heavenly. The warmth of his skin, the deepness of his voice, the intensity of his gaze . . . Perhaps Amelia had let her senses take over her brain, but she released his hand and slid both her hands up his chest. Grigg lifted his head, his brows raised.

Clearly she'd surprised him. She'd surprised herself. But she was done waiting for him to kiss her. So she'd take matters in her own hands. She wrapped her arms about his neck, then pressed her mouth against his and kissed Grigg Edison.

It took him a second to catch on, but once he did, he had her backed up against the wall in a flash. He trapped her between his body and the wall, and she wasn't complaining, because the way he was kissing made her feel like she needed to be held up. When he angled his mouth for a deeper kiss, she grasped his shirt to hold on.

She guessed that she'd assumed kissing Grigg would be great, even better than great. But this. This was amazing. His hands cradled her face, and she felt cherished and like he'd been waiting to kiss her for two years. Perhaps he had. And perhaps she had too.

Her mind buzzed, her heart hammered, and her body sang.

As his mouth moved over hers, claiming it again and again, she could only think of how she didn't want him to stop. Didn't want this to stop. And why had they waited so long?

It seemed they'd been dancing around each other forever, and could have been for much longer, if not for her list. One that she was definitely revamping tonight. Maybe she would burn it or shred it, because she was pretty sure Hayden and Jack, the two men left, would never kiss her like Grigg. Not that kissing and chemistry should be the indicator of a good relationship, but it was a darn good start.

The thought made her smile, and Grigg drew away, breathing hard. "What are you smiling about?"

She loved the feel of his body pressed against hers, the touch of his hands, the scent of him . . .

"Mills?" he whispered, placing a tiny kiss on her jaw, then another near her earlobe.

"I think you made the list."

He chuckled, his chest vibrating against hers. "I think you need to get rid of that list."

"Done."

He lifted his head and gazed into her eyes. "Really?"

She ran her fingers over the stubble of his jaw. "You can do the honors if you'd like."

A grin spread across his face, then he kissed her again on the mouth. Softly. It was over much too soon, but he grasped her hand and drew her along with him toward the kitchen.

"In a hurry, are we?" she teased.

"Where's the list?"

She released his hand and pulled it out of her computer bag. The first two names were crossed off, as well as Peter's. Only Hayden's and Jack's remained.

"What are you going to tell Hayden?" Grigg asked, looking at the list with her.

She shrugged. "I'll figure something out. Maybe I'll tell him I have shingles or something. He's a huge germaphobe."

"So he wanted to take you hiking? In nature?"

"Yeah. You should see the routine he goes through when hiking."

Grigg shook his head. "I don't think I want to know." Then he slipped his arm about her shoulder and leaned down and kissed her temple.

It was new, but it felt nice, this casual affection from Grigg.

"Here goes," he said, ripping the sheet of paper in half. He ripped it in half two more times. Then he crumpled it up and found her kitchen trash.

"Nice," she said, setting her hands on her hips. "I guess it's official then?"

"What's official?" he asked, his mouth curving as he walked toward her.

She took a step back, then another. "Don't tell me you've changed your mind."

"Never." He reached her and pulled her close.

Her heart started thumping again. Slowly, he moved his hands over her back as their bodies seemed to meld together. "What are you doing tomorrow?" he asked against her hair.

"You tell me."

She didn't have to look up at him to know he was smiling.

"I don't think I've ever heard a better phrase coming from you in two years."

Tilting her head up, she met his smiling gaze. "I'm a new woman, remember?"

"Yep." He leaned down and kissed her again. This kiss was not the frantic heat of the one in the hallway but slower, more thoughtful.

Warmth pooled in her belly, and she allowed herself to run her fingers over his shoulders, then behind his neck and into his hair. She could tell he was holding back, and she was grateful. The last thing she wanted to do was tell him it was time to leave.

"Mills," he whispered against her mouth. "I'll be here at seven tomorrow morning. Wear tennis shoes."

"Why?" she whispered back, stealing another kiss.

"It's a surprise," he said.

She drew back just enough to connect their gazes. "No wilderness stuff."

The edge of his mouth lifted. "There will be cell service, so you won't have to miss all your Sunday texts and emails that are so urgent."

"Ha. Ha."

"I've got your back, babe, don't forget it."

She liked that, very much. She slid her hands down his neck, then lower, until she rested them on his chest. "Okay, I'll be ready."

He moved his hands to grasp hers, then he released her and stepped away. She followed him to the front door, where she leaned against the doorframe and folded her arms as she watched him get into his SUV and drive away.

After she shut her door and locked it, she brought her hands to her hot cheeks. Oh boy. What had just happened? What had she just agreed to? She could still feel Grigg's presence, even though he'd left.

It was like his light, spicy scent lingered, his voice echoed, and his touch remained on her skin.

Tomorrow she'd call Hayden and break the news. And then maybe she'd update her sister Lauren as well.

12

Grigg was a few minutes early to pick up Amelia, so he swung by his usual coffee shop. Maggie was there, and the second she saw him she waved him over.

Well, this was interesting. They hadn't talked or texted since that date.

"Grigg," she said, "did you hear about Clint?"

He frowned. "Um, no, I haven't."

Her brow stayed furrowed. "He got in a car wreck later that day, after our double date. We'd swapped numbers, and he said he'd call me later that night. When he didn't, I texted him the next day."

"Wow, is he okay?"

"He will be," Maggie said. "Broke his shoulder and got a pretty good concussion."

Grigg exhaled. That sounded rough, and he was surprised that Amelia didn't know.

"Well, I'm glad he'll be okay," he told Maggie. "Sorry to hear about his injuries."

Maggie gave him a half smile. "I visited him at the hospital, and well, we've been sort of dating. I hope that doesn't put you in an awkward place with Amelia."

"No," Grigg said. "Not at all." He wasn't about to confess to Maggie about the progression of things between him and Amelia. "Next time you talk to Clint, tell him I wish him a speedy recovery."

"Will do," Maggie said. "Now, you want your usual coffee?"

"Of course."

When Grigg arrived at Amelia's place, he decided to wait to tell her about Clint. He wanted to figure *them* out first this morning, before bringing up her ex-boyfriend. Grigg parked in front of her condo and climbed out. He'd brought along some supplies for the cabin, but he didn't plan on working on anything today. Not with Amelia there. If he had a few hours with her, there was no way he'd waste it.

He was operating on little sleep, since his entire world had pretty much shifted last night. He could only hope that she hadn't changed her mind about him, so it was a relief when she opened her door with a smile.

"Hey," he said.

Her smirk was in full force. "Hey."

She wore jeans and tennis shoes. Her pale-blue shirt was lightweight cotton with tiny polka dots. The blue in the shirt made the blue in her eyes pop. And her lips. Well, she was definitely wearing lip gloss.

This moment he hadn't planned out. Did he pull her into his arms and greet her with a proper kiss, like he wanted to? Did he let her take the lead?

"Let me grab my purse," she said, then disappeared inside.

Well, that took that question out of the running. He waited in the doorway, catching a glimpse of the living room and, beyond, the hallway. The hallway of good memories now.

"What are you smiling about?" Amelia asked, returning.

He exhaled. "You."

Her brows lifted, and he liked that her hair was braided, hanging over one shoulder. It would give him something to tug. So he did, and he rested his other hand on her waist. She smelled of morning sunshine.

"You are not going to kiss me in front of the entire neighborhood," she said, playfully pushing against his chest.

He grabbed her hand and pulled her close again. "I'm not?"

Her blue gaze held his. "Nope."

He couldn't help the smile that spread to his face. "Then when, may I ask?"

"I'll let you know." She turned from him and pulled her door shut to lock it.

Watching her, loving the way she'd teased him, only made his heart swell. There was no doubt that he was completely falling for her, if he hadn't already.

"So." She turned around and grasped his hand.

Point one for him.

"Where are we going?"

"It's still a surprise, but don't worry. I think you'll like it."

She blinked up at him, studying his face. She was too close, too tempting, and he leaned down again. But she dodged him with a laugh, then tugged him by the hand along the walkway toward his SUV. He opened the door for her, and she climbed in and pulled it shut before he could slide past her reserve.

"All right," he said through the closed door, lifting his hands in defeat.

When he climbed into the driver's seat, she'd already buckled her seatbelt.

"Are you a breakfast person?" he asked. "I mean besides your usual smoothie and granola bar?"

She wrinkled her nose. "I'm good for a few hours."

"Alright, then we'll take the direct route."

He headed toward Morrison while Amelia fiddled with the radio. Grigg kept stealing glances at her, still marveling that they were actually doing this. Spending time together. Dating.

"You'd better not be taking me on a four-hour hike," she said. "I already turned down one man's offer for that."

Grigg laughed. "Um, no. You'll see." The closer they got to the turnoff for the cabin, the more he looked forward to her reaction. Of course, she was fairly wealthy and could probably buy a huge cabin for herself if she wanted. But he hoped she'd like his modest project.

She leaned forward once they turned onto the smaller side road. "Okay, this looks suspiciously like a hiking destination."

He reached over and grasped her hand. "Patience, woman. We're only seconds away from the great reveal."

When they turned the final bend and the two-story cabin came into view, Amelia said, "What is this? Your family's cabin?"

"No," he said. "My family lives in California, remember? This place is my ultimate weekend project."

She said nothing for a moment, just stared through the windshield. When he parked on the gravel driveway, he said, "Come on, I'll give you the tour."

Amelia climbed out of the car, scanning the grounds and the cabin. "This is amazing, Grigg."

"You should have seen it before," he said.

"How long have you been working on it?" She walked alongside him as they moved to the wide porch.

"Pretty much since I moved here," he said. "I bought it not long after we signed our deal."

He led her up the newly built steps—the porch still needed to be stained. He had sanded it all last week, and now it gleamed like new wood.

"Did you do all this?" She pointed out the long porch.

"So far," he said. "Although I'm not much good at electrical, so that kind of thing I'm going to have to hire out. But if it has to do with wood or basic contracting stuff, I can figure it out."

Amelia nodded, then walked along the porch. She paused and peered through one of the windows Grigg hadn't hung with drapes yet. Maybe he'd put in blinds. He hadn't decided which he wanted to do. Anyone standing on the porch could see directly into the cabin.

Probably not the most secure thing in the world, but it wasn't like he had any valuables or furniture inside, except for the table, a couple chairs, and an old couch he'd found at Goodwill.

Amelia turned to him with a smile. "So this is why you don't come into the office on the weekends."

"No, this is my excuse," he said, walking toward her. He stopped when he reached her, and he grasped her hand. She let him link their fingers. "I don't come into the office on the weekends because it's hard to be alone with you, when I know you're off-limits."

Her blue eyes scanned his face. "So you thought you would be too tempted to tell me to put you on my list?"

"You weren't even open to a list until recently," he said, squeezing her hand.

She gave him a sassy smile. Then she stepped even closer, and now more than their fingers were touching, and Grigg did not mind at all.

"Are you going to give me the tour?" she asked.

"Eventually," he said, rubbing his thumb over her fingers.

She raised her brows. "What does that mean?"

"It means that I've been waiting to kiss you since I picked you up this morning." He moved his free hand up her arm, over the curve of her shoulder, until he let his fingers linger against the smoothness of her neck.

Her eyes fluttered shut, and he lowered his mouth to hers. She tasted sweet, warm, and like a lazy Sunday. He was pleased that she responded to his kiss as if she had been waiting too. The breeze stirred about them, the leaves rustled on the trees a few yards away, and the only sounds and scents were from nature herself. Kissing Amelia was everything he had ever imagined, and more. When she ran her hands up his chest, over his shoulders, and behind his neck, he drew her closer. He wanted to stay in this moment for as long as possible.

"Are you okay with me kissing you on this porch?" he rasped against her skin.

"You definitely have my permission," she said, her lips curving into a smile. "Isn't this better anyway? Just the two of us? No neighbors, no cars, no distractions."

She was right. No distractions. Which probably meant that he needed a distraction. "I agree with you a hundred percent, babe." He ran his hands down her back and settled at her waist, still holding her close. "Now I can give you the tour."

She seemed to reluctantly draw away. He linked their hands again, then he led her to the front door, which he opened.

As they walked through the main level of the cabin, Grigg saw the place through her eyes. Yeah, it was rough, and there was a lot of work to still do, but things were coming along as well. The cabinets in the kitchen were completely refinished, and he had yet to pull up the flooring and replace it, but the counters were in good shape.

"Did you refinish these cabinets?" Amelia said, running a hand over the sanded and newly stained wood.

"I did," he said with a grin. He rather liked her in this place, touching the things he'd built.

Next he showed Amelia where he'd repaired parts of the wall. Soon he could start painting. They walked along the hallway and into the two rooms: one could act as bedroom, and maybe the other could be an office. One of the first things he'd done after buying this cabin was enlarge the windows. So now the daylight spilled through the large square windows, giving each room a spacious feel. Amelia released his hand and walked over to the window that overlooked a copse of trees. "This is beautiful," she said. "I'm surprised that you come back into the city after weekends."

"Well," Grigg started, "I don't have Wi-Fi up here yet, and I don't think my business partner would be too happy if I missed meetings at the firm."

Amelia turned from the window and leaned against the frame, a sweet smile on her face. "Your partner, huh? She sounds pretty demanding."

"Oh, she is." Grigg strode toward her, and she edged away, a smirk on her face.

He wasn't going to let her get away so easily, so he grabbed her by the waist and pulled her against him. Amelia laughed but made no effort to get away. In fact, she looped her arms about his neck, then leaned into him and rested her cheek against his chest. She'd gone quiet, and Grigg didn't mind. He simply slipped his arms more fully around her and held her close.

The sound of Amelia's phone ringing broke apart the mood. "You can get that," Grigg said.

Amelia sighed, then she stepped away from Grigg. She pulled her phone out of her pocket. "It's an unknown number again." She put the phone back into her pocket and grabbed his hand. "Show me the rest of the place. I'd love to see it."

So he spent the better part of the next hour walking through the cabin hand in hand with Amelia, explaining his renovations and future plans. He was surprised by a number of questions that Amelia asked him, as if she were truly interested. They headed outside to see the deck he'd built and the grooming he'd started on the backyard space.

Amelia wandered around, examining the landscape. Then she put her hands on her hips and said, "Where did you get all this talent?"

"Staining a deck takes no talent," he said.

"You've done a lot more than staining decks or painting walls," Amanda said. "This stuff is professional work."

Grigg shrugged. "You know my dad is a construction manager, right?"

Amelia glanced over at him. "Yeah, I guess I do remember that. So did you used to work for him?"

"Yeah, I did," he said. "It's kind of a sore topic, though. My dad wasn't happy when I didn't come home after college and join his business. With the NFL out of the picture, he was sure that would be my second choice."

Amelia kept her gaze on his face. "Really? Why did I think your parents were fully supportive of your career?"

"Well, they're definitely proud that I have a college education," he said. "But they didn't see a need for a master's. My playing football was the highlight for my dad. Good thing I liked it well enough that it became my passion as well." Grigg released a breath. "When I got injured, my parents were upset of course, but my dad said that there was a silver lining, because he believed I'd come back home."

"Instead, you decided to get a master's?"

He nodded, looking away from her.

"Yeah, I can see how your dad would want you to work for him," she said. "But it is kind of ridiculous when you think about it. We all have to live our own lives, and you're an amazing financial guru. So you obviously followed your talent."

"Well, maybe someday you can tell my dad that," he said.

"I have no problem telling your dad how amazing, talented, and too smart for your own good you are." She moved closer to him, gazing up at him with those blue eyes of hers. Then she slipped her fingers through his.

He drew her against him, then leaned down and kissed her forehead. Her eyes fluttered shut, and so he kissed her for real. The kiss was a languid, slow simmer, surrounded by the peacefulness of the trees and the sounds of nature.

Invariably, the modern world protested, and Amelia's cell phone rang.

"Do you usually get so many phone calls on Sunday mornings?" Grigg asked.

She dragged her fingers over his shoulders.

"Not exactly," she said. "Sometimes I'll hear from my family on Sundays, but even that is not too often." She released him and pulled her phone out of her pocket. "Unknown caller again."

"Maybe you should answer it then," Grigg said. "Sometimes unknown numbers can happen when someone's out of their normal area."

She accepted the call and said, "Amelia Ambrose here, can I help you?"

Grigg couldn't hear what the woman on the other end of the line was saying, but he had never seen Amelia go pale before, until now. Whoever the caller was, she didn't have good news. He placed a hand on Amelia's shoulder, hoping to give her support in whatever it was.

When she hung up and met his gaze, the fear in her eyes made his stomach feel like it had been hollowed out.

13

AMELIA COULDN'T CATCH a normal breath. The woman on the phone wasn't making any sense. She'd identified herself as Hayden Black's mother, but the words coming from her mouth were like a nightmare.

"He's in the hospital," the woman said. "Collapsed at the funeral home. Just like that. As he was being wheeled away on a stretcher, he asked me to call his girlfriend. Imagine my surprise that Hayden had a girlfriend."

Amelia exhaled very carefully. "How's Hayden, Mrs. Black? Will he be all right?"

"Nobody knows," Mrs. Black said, her voice cracking. "I couldn't leave my mother's own funeral, you know. And the doctor said they're running tests."

"Okay, that's good, right?" Amelia said.

"Hayden wants you to come right away," Mrs. Black said.

Amelia wanted to say, *you're kidding,* but this was a distraught mother. "How about I call first to check up on him? Would that be all right?"

Mrs. Black huffed out a breath. "A girlfriend would care more. He said that you would want to see him and watch over him while he's in the hospital."

Amelia felt sorry for Hayden, whatever had happened to him, but the worry in her gut was for another reason. A much more serious reason. "I'll call him right now, and if you get any updates, please let me know."

When Amelia hung up, she felt Grigg's gaze on her. "That was Hayden's mom," she said in a slow voice. "He had some sort of collapse at the funeral home. He's undergoing testing at the hospital."

Finally she looked up at Grigg. The furrow between his brows was enough to tell her that he was worried about something beyond Hayden. "Call him, see how he's doing."

So with Grigg pacing the deck while she wandered the backyard, she called Hayden's cell phone. He answered on the third ring with a raspy, "Amelia, I'm glad you called."

"Hi." Her throat was a lump. "Your mother got ahold of me. How are you?"

"Truthfully, not good," he said. "They've found a massive blood clot in my leg, and they're putting a stent in this afternoon. Then I'll be on blood thinners and need to go to regular checkups to keep an eye on the thing."

"Oh, wow, that sounds awful," she said. "I'm glad you're getting the right help."

"Yeah," Hayden said. "I could have died. If everyone hadn't acted so fast to get me medical treatment, I would've been a goner."

The information was sobering to say the least.

"I'm so relieved." Amelia looked over to where Grigg was examining something on the outside of the cabin. But she wasn't fooled. She was pretty sure he could hear her entire side of the conversation.

"How long will you be in the hospital?" she asked Hayden.

"Probably at least two more nights," he said. "I told my mother to let you know that I'll need some help. You could come out here and then fly back to Denver with me. I probably shouldn't travel alone."

Alone, with more than a hundred other passengers on the plane. Amelia closed her eyes. She should think more generous thoughts. But she wasn't Hayden's girlfriend, and now she'd never be. A single date and a few phone calls didn't equate to her flying to be at his side like a serious girlfriend or wife.

"I'll talk things over with your mom," she said, for some reason unable to tell him no directly, at least at this moment. He was about to have surgery, and she didn't want to drop the information on him that she was in fact dating someone else now.

Because after all that had happened with Grigg in the past twenty-four hours, they'd better be dating.

"My mom already agrees," Hayden said. "I'd offer to pay for your airline ticket, but I know you're loaded."

Amelia cringed. Hayden knew she did well at her financial firm, but he didn't know about her millionaire-inheritance roots.

"I'll be in touch," she said. "And I'm so sorry—"

"You'd better not be ditching me," he said, his voice rising. "Like you did before. I almost died, Amelia, *died*."

She knew. All the compassion and pity and guilt fled immediately. She took a couple of even, steady breaths. "I hope everything goes well with your surgery, Hayden. I'll be in touch with your mom." She hung up before he could reply.

She didn't know what to say. But she did know that she wouldn't be flying to California. She should probably call Mrs. Black and more fully explain the situation. But she'd do that later, after Hayden's surgery.

Grigg was waiting, and she joined him on the deck. His gaze seemed troubled.

"Did you catch enough of it?" she asked, folding her arms.

"I did," he said, "and there's something I need to tell you. All this going on with Hayden reminded me."

Amelia frowned. "Okay . . ."

"Before I picked you up this morning, I stopped for coffee," he said. "Maggie was there."

She had no idea where he was going with bringing up Maggie.

"After our double date that day, Clint was in a car accident."

Amelia gasped. "No."

Grigg's nod was somber. "He's fine, or he will be fine. He broke something in his shoulder and ended up with a concussion. It seems that he and Maggie are officially dating now."

Amelia continued to stare at Grigg, her mind whirling.

"That's . . ." She closed her eyes because it was too painful to look at the man she was going to have to break up with. "That's too much of a coincidence. Both of them injured soon after contact with me."

He closed the distance between them and set his hands on her shoulders.

"I know what you're thinking, Mills, and none of this is your fault."

She swallowed back the pain, but it didn't go anywhere.

"Besides," he continued in a quiet voice, "Clint's was a freak accident, but with Hayden, blood clots don't develop overnight."

She couldn't think straight. All she knew was that her pulse was racing and her stomach felt like it had been turned inside out.

"Come inside, out of the sun," Grigg said, steering her through the back door.

She followed numbly. Clint had been in a car accident. The same day they'd gone to lunch. And now only a week after she'd gone on a date with Hayden . . .

"Drink this," Grigg said, grasping her hand and placing a water bottle in it.

She hadn't even comprehended that she had sat on the single piece of furniture in the cabin—an old couch—and Grigg had gotten her a drink.

She stared at the label on the water bottle. Was the water really from a glacier? What kind of job would that be? It must take special equipment to get up a mountainside and haul glacier ice back and forth. And surely they purified it somehow. Did that compromise the pH balance?

"Mills," Grigg said. "Have a drink."

She took a sip of the water, then handed it back to Grigg. She wasn't thinking straight, she knew that. But the evidence was before her. "It's the curse."

Grigg took her hand. "No—"

"It has to be." She snatched her hand from his and pushed off the couch. She paced the cabin floor. "It's too much of a sign."

"When you dated those men before, there were no accidents," he said, rubbing a hand over the back of his neck. "How do you explain that? I'll tell you. This is only a coincidence. Nothing to do with the curse. Besides, you said yourself that it's breakable."

She turned to him and stared at the man that she'd began to have so much hope for, and with. "It is breakable, but it can obviously still control things. As we've seen with Clint and Hayden. I don't know how to break it for myself. My sisters did it, but *I* haven't. Not yet." Her chest burned, and her eyes stung. The tears were coming, fast.

Amelia had to leave. Had to get back home. Call Lauren or even Sofia. Figure out what was happening.

Grigg rose from the couch, and before she could open the front door, he drew her against him. "Hey," Grigg said in a soft voice against her hair. His arms were strong, warm, comforting, but that only scared her more.

If anything happened to Grigg . . .

A sob choked in her throat, and she buried her face against his chest, taking solace and comfort in him one more time. Because after today, she didn't know what would happen.

Grigg merely held her, moving one hand slowly along her back as she cried.

None of this was fair, and although she'd lived with the curse her entire life, it had never hurt so bad as it did now.

"Babe, we'll figure this out, I promise."

She shook her head, and his arms only tightened about her. "Don't you see?" she choked out. "This means I'm back to square one. We can't date. We can't be together at all, except for work. Maybe I've already jinxed that too."

Grigg didn't argue, and he didn't pull away. He simply let her ramble about all of her worries.

"I'm sorry," she said at last. "This isn't fair to you." She drew away, wiping at her eyes. "I think it's best that we just call things off right now. Before things go farther. Before hearts get involved."

"It's too late for that." Grigg smoothed back her hair and kissed her temple. "Come on, let's get out of here. I have a plan."

She tugged his hand to stop before they could leave the cabin. "What do you mean you have a plan? That's exactly what this curse is—it will screw up any plans."

Grigg opened the cabin door, then looked down at her. "I think we need to go to your hometown. Talk to your grandmother in person. Find out the root of this curse and what it can do and can't do. Then, once and for all, get rid of it."

Amelia released a slow breath. Grigg's suggestion made sense, yet she couldn't let him come with her. That would just mean more time together, which would only make it harder to let him go. "Maybe you're right. But I need to go alone."

"You're not going alone," he said. "You can fly alone if you want, but I'll be showing up at Ambrose too."

She blinked back a fresh round of tears.

Grigg folded his arms. "I'm being serious."

"I know you are." She wanted to throw her arms around his neck, but she only said, "Thank you, Grigg."

He nodded. Then he locked up the cabin, and they walked to the SUV together.

As they drove down the canyon road, silence fell between them. Amelia hated the curse. She hated that she was born into the Ambrose family. If she could trade the curse for every penny of her inheritance, she would in a heartbeat, because that would mean she could have the man beside her.

When they reached the city and stopped at a traffic light, she said, "I'm sorry for being the worst date ever and ruining the tour of your beautiful property."

Grigg reached for her hand and threaded his fingers through hers.

Amelia's heart leapt at the contact, but she tamped down the hope for a future between them before it could take solid root in her heart.

"I'm not going anywhere, Mills, even if you never let me kiss you again."

She turned her head to meet his gaze. She felt like crying again, but she swallowed back the surfacing emotion. "You really don't have to come with me," she said in a quiet voice.

The light turned green, and Grigg accelerated. "I want to come. I want answers as much as you do."

Amelia nodded and focused on the road again. Maybe, just maybe, they could get to the bottom of the curse once and for all.

14

A FREAK RAINSTORM delayed their flight, so when Grigg and Amelia deplaned in the small airport near Ambrose, Texas, it had already been a long day. They'd waited a week so that they didn't have to cancel any immediate meetings. And they hadn't booked a return flight, but if everything went smoothly, Grigg expected the trip to take only two to three days. At least that's what he had told Amelia to ease her stress about leaving the office for too long.

As they walked to the baggage claim, Grigg said, "It's pretty late. Maybe we should rent a car or take a taxi."

"It's okay," Amelia said, stifling a yawn. "Shelton will be here. I texted him right before we took off."

Amelia had explained that her grandmother had a personal chauffeur, William Shelton. But he was an older gentleman, and now that it was almost midnight, Grigg worried they were interrupting the man's sleep.

But, true to Amelia's word, a dark sedan was waiting outside the airport for them at the curb. William Shelton climbed out. He was bald, but Grigg guessed he shaved his head, because the man couldn't be too much older than mid-sixties. With a slight limp, Shelton met Grigg at the trunk. The two men shook hands, then Shelton embraced Amelia.

"It's been too long, darlin'," Shelton told her. "What's kept you away?"

"I opened my own investment firm in Denver," Amelia told him. "Didn't Grandma tell you?"

Shelton gave her a sheepish smile. "Perhaps. There's a lot to keep track of with Ambrose Estate. All I know is that it's wonderful to see you."

Once they were all loaded into the car, Grigg insisted that Amelia sit in the passenger seat, and the smooth car hummed along the dark roads. Grigg had never been to this part of Texas, and he'd be interested to see it in the daylight.

"You've come about the curse, haven't you?" Shelton asked Amelia.

"How did you know?"

"Your grandmother told me just an hour ago, and my memory's not that bad."

Amelia smiled at the older gentleman. "Yes, we've come about the curse."

"He must be someone special."

Amelia laughed. "He is special." Then she looked back at Grigg and winked.

Well, then. Grigg could definitely be on board with this. When they pulled into a long drive edged by trees on either side, leading to a gorgeous three-story mansion, Grigg released a low whistle.

"When was this place built?" he asked.

"1890s is what I've been told," Amelia said.

"You grew up here?" he said. A massive lawn led up to the house that was positioned on top of a rising slope. To one side was a four-car garage.

"Not full-time," Amelia said. "By the time my mom had me, she was on her second husband, and we moved around a lot."

Grigg had heard about her father's death when she was a kid.

Shelton pulled to a stop on the circular driveway in front of the elegant double doors of the house. "Let's get your luggage out here, then I'll go park the car."

"Sounds good, thanks." Amelia opened her door, and Grigg climbed out too.

Outside, Grigg was able to take in the expanse of the place. The moon was nearly full and cast a glowing web across the white house and the surrounding grounds. Fifteen thousand acres, Amelia had told him. The size was staggering, but here in Texas, it seemed everything really was bigger. As Grigg picked up the two carry-ons and walked with Amelia up the front steps, he said, "This place is gorgeous."

"Wait until you see inside." Amelia reached for the doorknob to open the door.

He followed her into a spacious hall, with a crystal chandelier glowing above, lighting the curved staircase beyond. The wood floors gleamed, and the rugs were plush and elegant. The interior was stately.

No one was there to greet them, and Grigg wasn't surprised. He assumed Amelia's grandmother had been in bed for hours. But then a voice spoke from somewhere above.

"Is that you, Millie dear?"

By the elderly tone, Grigg thought it could only be her grandmother.

"Gran," Amelia took the steps two at a time. "Don't come down. We'll come up. Where's Mrs. B?"

Earlier, Amelia had explained that Mrs. Beatrice O'Connor was the longtime housekeeper at the estate. The woman had worked for Mrs. Ambrose since the 1970s.

Grigg trudged after Amelia, carrying the bags. At the second-story landing, a woman came into view. She was taller than Grigg had expected, and her wrinkles bespoke her age, but her blue eyes were full of life and vigor.

"Beatrice is already asleep," the woman said. "I decided to wait up." When her gaze moved past Amelia to Grigg, Mrs. Ambrose smiled.

Amelia grasped her grandmother's hands just then and kissed the woman's cheek.

"Well, let's have a look at the both of you," Mrs. Ambrose said.

Grigg set down the bags and stepped forward, intent on shaking her hand. But she kept one hand on her cane and the other clutching her navy silk robe to her throat.

"How old are you, young man?"

This was unexpected, but Amelia had warned him that her grandmother could be a bit odd.

"I'm twenty-eight." He glanced at Amelia, who looked both relieved and exhausted. Was it a good thing to be asked his age by her grandmother?

Mrs. Ambrose looked him over from head to foot, yet Grigg didn't mind.

Her blue eyes reminded him of Amelia's, and it was clear that this woman was used to commanding attention and being in charge.

"Welcome to Ambrose, Mr. Edison," she said, holding out her hand.

Grigg reached her hand and gave it a gentle shake, but her fingers wrapped around his tightly.

"Now, listen to me, young man," she said in a whisper.

Amelia was standing right next to them, so Grigg didn't know why Mrs. Ambrose was whispering.

"Whatever you do, take care of my Millie," Mrs. Ambrose said. "She hasn't had an easy day in her life, and I don't want any more heartache to come her way. Do you hear me?"

"Yes, ma'am," Grigg said. "I promise to take care of your granddaughter." Oddly, this felt like a formal meeting between a beau and a woman's parent. Like a test of some sort. Also, his mind was spinning with questions about what Mrs. Ambrose was specifically talking about when she brought up Amelia's heartache. Was the elderly woman referring to the early death of Amelia's father? Her absent mother?

He knew some of these things, but Amelia rarely talked about either of her parents, or her half sisters for that matter.

Mrs. Ambrose was still grasping his hand. "She must never take off her pendant, do you understand?"

Grigg's throat went dry. "I understand."

"Gran, you don't need to—"

She still wasn't finished. "Young man," she said in a pointed voice, "at Ambrose, family comes first, always has."

"Understood," Grigg said.

Finally Mrs. Ambrose released her hold on him, and truth be told Grigg felt a bit unsteady.

"We'll see you at breakfast in the morning, Grandma," Amelia said, giving her grandmother another kiss on the cheek. "We didn't mean to keep you waiting up for us."

Her grandmother smiled, her gaze warming again. "Be sure to keep your door shut and locked, Millie. You don't want temptation to set in."

"Grigg is a perfect gentleman," Amelia said, her tone bordering on laughter.

They waited a few moments while Mrs. Ambrose shuffled down the hallway, then Amelia whispered, "Follow me."

He walked with her along the opposite hallway, away from the direction that Mrs. Ambrose had gone. Amelia opened a door about halfway down the hall and flipped on a light.

He peered in. The bedroom was spacious and elegant. A king-sized bed stood in the center, draped in a royal-blue bedspread. The tall windows also had the same color drapes, and a stately cherrywood armoire stood in the corner of the room next to another door.

"That's a walk-in closet," Amelia said. "There's another door inside, and it leads to my closet."

"The rooms adjoin?"

"Not in the traditional sense." She nudged him. "Don't get any ideas, or my grandmother will kick you out."

"Too late for that."

Amelia playfully slapped his arm, and he caught her hand, then drew her close.

Over the past week, they'd only spent a few stolen moments together. They hadn't even gone on what Grigg would deem an official date. Amelia had forbidden it, paranoid that a date or even the planning of a date would lead to him ending up in the hospital like Clint and Hayden. She'd texted Hayden that she had some work issues and a family emergency, so she wouldn't be able to come to California. She still hadn't found the time or the gumption to call him in person and tell him that there would be no second date.

Grigg was quite happy with him being the last man standing, so to speak. He'd even stolen a couple of kisses from her at work. Both times, she'd had to end it much too soon.

This time, though, Amelia didn't shoo him away. She wrapped her arms about his waist and leaned into him. He pulled her close and buried his face in her hair as he slowly stroked her back. He loved that she'd hugged him, and he loved that she had allowed him to come to Ambrose. Her body was warm and soft against his, and the last thing he wanted to do tonight was let her go.

"I don't know about all of this," Amelia murmured. "My grandmother can be intimidating, and she's very protective of her granddaughters. Are you sure you want to be here?"

He kissed the top of her head. "I'm sure. Are you sure you'll be okay in that room by yourself?"

She lifted her head to meet his gaze. "You made a promise to my grandma."

He tapped the end of her nose. "I did. But know that I'm on the other side of the door if you need anything. Anything at all."

She nodded, her eyes glistening. This was the real reason Grigg had wanted to come. He'd never seen Amelia so fragile before. And since receiving the news about Hayden's health, Grigg had been worried about Amelia herself. The last thing he wanted her to do was give up, throw away hope, or dismiss the idea that there could be a future between them.

"So what's the first item on our agenda, Miss Ambrose?"

"Sofia sent me a to-do list," she said. "First thing is to look through some old journals. Sofia said that will help me understand the beginning of it all, so that I can then figure out how to put a stop to all of this insanity once and for all."

"Sounds good to me." Grigg said. "We'll find the answers, I know it."

Her blue eyes held his. "I hope so, I really do."

An hour later, Grigg was still awake, standing at the bedroom window that overlooked the back gardens, where a pool glistened in the moonlight and a graveyard cast inky shadows beyond. The place was stately and beautiful, but from the moment Shelton had turned onto the driveway leading to the mansion, Grigg had sensed the forlornness of the place.

There was no doubt this place had secrets, and some might be unpleasant to uncover.

15

AMELIA GAZED AT her reflection in the mirror in the early-morning light. The mirror didn't lie. She looked as stressed as she felt, with the puffiness of her eyes and her pale cheeks. On one hand, she couldn't believe that she was back at Ambrose; on the other, since arriving, she'd felt a sense of doom.

Maybe it was because Gran had seemed so much older suddenly. Yes, the woman was in her late eighties, but she'd always been so stoic and timeless. But now . . . Gran was frail, and the violet circles under her eyes told Amelia that her grandmother wasn't as spry as she used to be. The thought was sobering. Some months ago, Gran had surprised everyone and left the entire estate and surrounding lands to Sofia.

As Sofia was the oldest granddaughter, it had made sense. Well, unless you asked their mother, Poppy. She hadn't been pleased, but an offer of more money had appeased her for the time being. The rest of the granddaughters still had their trust funds that paid out monthly allowances, and they still owned equity in the holding company.

But returning to Ambrose, and with Grigg no less, had made everything all the more real. Amelia had always felt the weight of the curse, even back when her half sisters had each received the Pendant of Protection on their sixteenth birthdays. And that weight had doubled when Amelia received her own pendant. In fact, after that, Amelia had rarely visited Ambrose again.

And now she was back.

She heard the sounds of movement coming from the bedroom belonging to Grigg. So he was awake early too. She probably shouldn't go bursting through the dressing room to greet him. No, she'd have to be much more civilized and formal. It had been hard enough to leave him last night and to know that he was just on the other side of the wall.

That knowledge had sent her heart racing for more than one reason. She didn't want to be apart from Grigg, not even for a night, and that thought alone made her more scared than ever. She'd become attached to him. Long before their flirting turned more serious. She realized now, looking back, that only a couple of months into their working together, she'd come to rely on him for so many things. Not only for work-related needs but emotional needs, and as a friend that she'd never really had.

A light tap sounded at her closet door.

Amelia turned from the mirror. Grigg had come through the dressing room himself to knock on *her* door. She couldn't help the smile that spread across her face. After hurrying to the closet door, she opened it.

Her eyes widened, and her pulse drummed hot. Grigg stood there wearing board shorts . . . and that was it. There was no doubt that he was a former athlete who still prioritized staying in shape.

He hadn't even gotten dressed properly, and now he was in her bedroom, smiling at her.

"Good morning," he said in a morning voice she hadn't heard before.

She really, really liked it.

"Hey, what are you doing?" she asked, because he was tugging her toward the windows of her bedroom, a lazy smile on his face.

"I'm showing you something," he said, then he stopped and pointed.

The back gardens sparkled with dew in the morning light, and the greens of the bushes and trees, intermingling with the vibrant colors of the flowers, were breathtaking. The swimming pool was turquoise, surrounded by pale-gray stone slabs. Pristine and untouched.

"Let's go swimming," Grigg said. "You brought your suit, right? You told me to."

"I did," Amelia said, sneaking a glance at him. "I didn't know you were such an avid swimmer—especially so early in the morning."

"I think I need to get rid of some energy." He slid his warm hand across her neck, then leaned close and placed the softest of kisses on her jaw. The bare skin of his torso brushed against her arm, and Amelia knew that a swim in the cool water of the pool would be just the thing to refocus her brain on why they'd come to Ambrose.

"Okay, I'll be ready in a few." She should really move away from him, right now. But she couldn't resist. So she turned toward him and rose up on her toes to kiss him. Of course, that meant that she had to place her hand on his chest for balance.

Grigg kissed her slowly like he had all the time in the world, not pulling her closer but simply running his hands along her back.

"You need to leave now," she said, trying to catch her breath.

He winked, then nodded. She watched him walk to the door that connected to the hallway. "I'll be waiting out here."

"All right," she said in a voice that sounded too high.

When he pulled the door shut, she moved to her carry-on suitcase. She hadn't even unpacked the night before. She dug through her clothes and located her plain black swimsuit. Boring, maybe, but she rarely swam, and she hadn't really thought through this scenario. Even though she'd told Grigg to bring his.

Now, suddenly in the light of the morning, she felt self-conscious. Once she was wearing a swimming suit, there would be nothing to hide from Grigg. Not that she had poor body image, but what Grigg thought of her mattered. And she didn't think he was shallow by any means. No, it would only put them in more intimate circumstances.

Don't be a ninny, she told herself. She quickly changed and didn't even check her image in the mirror but grabbed a towel from the adjoining bathroom and wrapped it around her waist. Then she stepped into the hallway. The house was quiet and dim, and there was Grigg. Waiting.

No interference from Gran this time, or anyone else who might be about the house.

He only smiled and grasped her hand.

Together they walked down the main stairs, then out the French doors that led to the back gardens and the swimming pool.

The air was warming, and it would be quite hot that afternoon, but right now, it was pretty much perfect. As they neared the pool, Amelia expected Grigg to let go of her hand, but he didn't. Instead, he pulled her with him and wrapped an arm about her waist. "Ready?" he asked, unhooking her towel.

She grasped the towel to keep it on. "I'm not jumping in," she said. "It's probably cold, so that means I need to get used to it inch by inch."

"Suit yourself." He released her, then did a perfect dive into the pool.

She backed up to avoid any splashing, then she watched as he swam to the other side of the pool, deftly and swiftly. If she hadn't known he was a former football player, she would have guessed him to be a swimmer. His strokes were even and perfect, and when he turned to swim back toward her, she clapped.

He came up out of the water when he reached her side again. Wet was definitely a nice look on him. He held out a hand. "Come on. The water's nice."

"I think I'll just watch you," she said, taking a step back. "I can float, that's pretty much it."

His brows rose. "I thought you'd swim more, growing up here."

"I only visited here a few times as a teen," she said. "And my mom was always too preoccupied with whoever she was dating to take me to extra things like swimming lessons. So I'm more of a shallow-water type of girl, or lying out on the pool chairs."

"I think we need to change that," he said. "A woman who runs a successful financial firm needs to be able to swim as well. You know, in case we throw a pool party."

She scoffed. "Funny."

He grasped the edge of the pool and hauled himself out of the water.

Amelia backed up a couple of steps, to get out of his way, but he reached her too fast.

"Come on, I'll teach you a few things," he said, his hand wrapped around her wrist and his wet torso dangerously close to hers. "You'll be swimming before you know it."

Grigg this close, wet, and only wearing his board shorts was pretty much impossible to resist.

She took a deep breath. "Okay."

"Okay?" He grinned.

She nodded.

Then before she could change her mind, he tugged her towel free and tossed it toward a chair. Then he led her to the edge of the pool. "We'll jump together, because it's much easier to get wet all at once."

"I don't think—"

But he jumped, and she was still holding his hand, so seconds later she plunged into the water. The cold was sudden and fierce but, by the time she surfaced, not nearly as bad as she thought it would be.

Grigg hooked an arm about her waist and drew her close. "That wasn't so bad, was it?"

Still catching her breath, she said, "I don't know. I think I'm in shock."

He chuckled, then with his other hand he steered them to the edge of the swimming pool. "Hang on with both hands and watch me for a second. Then I'll have you try it."

She watched his effortless strokes, which were probably helped by his powerful shoulders, his muscled arms, and his lithe torso. None of which she possessed.

"Okay, your turn," he said, turning and swimming back to her.

He guided her into position, gave her some pointers on breathing. Then he swam alongside of her, helping her adjust when she had to pause. They made three laps, and by then she was completely out of breath.

"I think I'm ready to lounge on a pool chair now," she said.

"You're just getting the hang of it." Grigg said, moving a wet lock of hair from her face. His fingers trailed along her cheek, and the water was no longer cold. "Come on, at least one more lap."

Amelia bit the bottom of her lip and looked across the length of the pool. "I'm not in shape like you."

"You're in plenty good shape," he said. "You're just not used to swimming." He drew her with him toward the middle of the pool. "Okay, on your back. We'll do the backstroke the rest of the way. It's not far."

Amelia leaned back and felt the pressure of Grigg's hand on her lower back, holding her up. She followed his instructions again, and strangely, she enjoyed the backstroke. Probably because she didn't have to keep putting her face in the water.

When they reached the far edge of the pool, she said, "Go do your thing, Grigg. I'll be cheering for you."

He chuckled, then kissed the tip of her nose. Before her mind could catch up to his actions, he pushed off the wall and began to swim laps. She stopped counting after about ten laps. How long was he going to swim?

Not that she wasn't enjoying watching his powerful body slicing through the water. Every few laps, he angled to her and kissed her again. She'd laugh and push him away. Then he stopped at the other end of the pool and draped his arms along the edge, catching his breath.

"Worn out already?" she teased.

He grinned. "I think you should backstroke over here. You've had enough of a break."

She raised her brows.

"Come on, Mills," he said. "I'll make it worth your while."

"Oh yeah? How?"

"Trust me."

She already did, she realized. Had for a long time. The realization only made her heart thump harder. After a slow exhale, she turned and pushed herself off the wall and began the backstroke across the pool. She could hear Grigg's encouragement, and she was proud of herself for not stopping.

Then she bumped into Grigg before reaching the wall.

He turned her to face him, and with one hand, she grasped the edge of the pool.

"You made it," he said.

She'd also gone at an angle rather than straight across. "Wow, how did that happen?"

"You're using more muscles on one side of your body," he said.

"I don't have muscles to use," she said with a laugh. "Hope you're not disappointed."

"Now, why would I want to be with a woman who was all muscle?" He inched closer, slipping both hands around her waist.

"You probably shouldn't state your intentions too loudly," she whispered. "Remember where we are."

"I remember," he said, his dark-brown eyes warm. He pulled her closer. "I feel rebellious, though."

She laughed and covered his mouth with her hand. "I'm not kidding, Grigg."

He moved her hand and kissed her. She held onto him and kissed him back while he kept them afloat in the water. The warmth of the sun spreading across the pool contrasted with the cool water, causing goose bumps to break out all over Amelia's skin.

Amelia was in danger of losing her heart completely to this man, that she knew. Their physical affection was a new thing, but it felt completely natural and only left her wanting to be around Grigg every moment of every day.

When she drew away, she sighed. "Too bad we have to get back to reality."

"I'm planning on cracking that curse today."

"If only . . ." She didn't finish, because she couldn't.

He seemed to understand, and he guided her across the pool. After climbing out of the water first, he held out her towel so she could step into it immediately.

After she wrapped up in the towel, he moved her hair to the side and kissed the side of her neck.

She closed her eyes, soaking in the almost-perfect moment of the nearness of Grigg, the warmth of the morning sun drying her skin, and the peaceful stillness of the garden beyond.

The double French doors opened at the back of the house, and a woman stepped out. By the silver-and-black hair and the woman's stout frame, Amelia knew it was the housekeeper.

Mrs. B spoke first. "Come quickly. Your grandmother's in a state, and I can't calm her down."

Amelia strode around the pool. "What's happened? Is she sick?"

"No," Mrs. B said, reaching for Amelia's hands and gripping them. "Your grandmother just had word that Poppy will be here this afternoon."

Amelia's mouth nearly fell open. She hadn't seen or spoken to her mother in over two years, since right before Amelia opened the firm in Denver. They'd had a major falling-out, and it had been the push that Amelia needed to completely set out on her own.

She'd never told anyone but her grandmother the truth behind the estrangement. No matter how much time passed, the last person Amelia ever wanted to see was her mother.

16

"I TAKE IT you're not too happy to see your mom?" Grigg asked as they crossed the wide lawn, heading toward the Ambrose family cemetery.

Amelia had spent some time with her distraught grandmother, then the matriarch had wanted to be alone. So Grigg had suggested they explore the estate while they waited for Poppy to show up.

Grigg was actually quite intrigued to check out the cemetery and read the grave markers. Determine for himself the threads of the curse that wove through the family. And right now, Amelia was walking faster than necessary. Stomping, really.

Grigg followed, waiting for Amelia to work through her churning emotions. She finally slowed and turned. The shade of the massive trees that towered over the garden path kept things cool, but a light sheen of perspiration dotted her forehead. Her blue eyes were stormy, and Grigg rested his hands on her shoulders. "Hey, what's wrong? I know you said the two of you don't have much contact, but you never told me why."

Amelia looked away and bit the edge of her lip. It was obvious that whatever she was going through with her mom was painful. Then she leaned forward and wrapped her arms about Grigg. He didn't know what was going on, but he was more than fine to offer her comfort if that was all she wanted.

He rubbed her back, and she nestled closer.

Above, the leaves of the trees clattered in the breeze, and the humming of insects could be heard coming from the flowering bushes along the path. Otherwise, the silence dominated. From his viewpoint, he could see the gated cemetery and the gray headstones sprouting from the green grass.

When Amelia finally pulled away, she clasped Grigg's hand and walked toward the cemetery. "Come on, I want to show you something," she said in a faint voice.

He followed easily, linking their fingers. They entered the cemetery, and she continued to draw him by the hand until they stood by one of the newer headstones. The name on it read: *Lyle Sorenson.* The death date was just over eight years ago.

"That's my father," she said.

Grigg blinked, then looked down at her. "I thought he'd died when you were a little kid."

Amelia's fingers tightened around his. "I did too."

"What do you mean?"

"When I was seven years old, my mom told me my father had died," Amelia said. "They'd split a few months before, and she was already dating another man by then."

The sadness in her voice was way too fresh for something that had happened so long ago.

"I remember my entire world shifted," she said. "No longer was I waiting for my daddy to come visit like some of the other kids of divorced parents. But now, he'd never come."

Grigg exhaled, still not fully understanding. The date on the headstone before them belied what Amelia was telling him.

"It was family custom to spend the week after your sixteenth birthday at the Ambrose Estate. Since my birthday is in May, I didn't arrive until June, when summer break started." She leaned her head against Grigg's shoulder.

"You always took school seriously, even at that age."

"Right," Amelia said. "Gran gave me the Pendant of Protection, which I didn't think too much about at the time. We all knew about the curse, of course, but Gran always called it poppycock, although I suspected she was just putting on a brave face so as to not worry the rest of us. I think my mom was more afraid of the curse than Gran."

Amelia went quiet for a moment, then said, "Like all teen girls, I wanted to get tan. So I spent most of the time by the pool during my birthday week at Ambrose. Not swimming, of course, I wasn't much good at that."

She squeezed his hand, and he squeezed back.

She took a deep breath, then continued. "So you can imagine my surprise when I fell asleep and then awakened to overhearing a phone conversation. My mom was talking to someone on her phone as she walked along a garden path on the other side of the swimming pool. Out of my sight, but I could still hear her voice."

Grigg didn't comment, just listened.

"So . . . she was talking to a doctor, it seemed. About *my dad*. Who had been dead for years." The surprise he felt probably didn't compare to the shock she'd had that sunny day. "It seemed that my dad hadn't died when I was a little kid. He had recently died, which meant that for years he'd been alive and I had no idea."

Grigg rubbed at his face and blew out a breath.

Amelia released his hand and moved away, folding her arms. "I was shocked to say the least, and then I confronted my mom. Do you know what she said?"

"Tell me." Grigg tried to keep his voice calm, even.

She blinked rapidly. "Poppy told me he was dead to *her*, and that she didn't want to deal with a whiney kid asking to see her dad all of the time." She covered her mouth and closed her eyes.

Grigg was at her side in an instant. He pulled her into his arms, and she sagged against him.

"I spent so many nights crying over my dad when I first lost him," she whispered. "Then the second time . . . I went numb."

Grigg made slow circles over her back as she clung to him. "Come on," he said. "Let's sit down. You can tell me what you remember about your dad."

Grigg sat on one of the benches with her, holding her hand, while she told him how her dad had been her favorite person in the entire world. How her mom had always been busy with her three older half sisters when Amelia was little, then how, when her dad had left, Poppy started dating again.

From that point on, Poppy's life had revolved around whichever new man she was dating. "Then she married again and had my twin half sisters, Kendra and Katelynn." Amelia shrugged. "I'd learned to become pretty independent anyway, so I continued on with how I was already living."

Grigg smoothed a bit of her hair back and kissed her temple. "You're the most independent woman I know," he said. "And I know your childhood and teen years were really hard, but I'm glad I know you now."

Amelia leaned her head against Grigg's shoulder. "Well, except for my crying jag just now, I'm usually more put together."

Grigg chuckled. "You don't have to tell me that you've a spine of steel, Amelia Ambrose. Don't forget I'm your business partner."

She wrapped both of her arms about him, and Grigg rested his chin on top of her head. He wanted to make this better for her, to ease her pain somehow.

When her stomach grumbled, he said, "Hungry? We should go into town and get breakfast."

She lifted her head. "Mrs. B will be mortally offended if we don't eat her breakfast."

"Oh, she's made something?"

A smile peeked through Amelia's sorrow. "Wait until you see. I think you'll be happy."

Sure enough, Mrs. B had set out a breakfast buffet, and Grigg was glad they hadn't gone anywhere to breakfast. He ate two platefuls of food, even though Amelia told him that lunch would be just as good.

"It's not fair that men like you can eat to your heart's content and not put on weight like women do," she told him as she eyed all the food piled onto his plate.

"I hope you're not talking about yourself, Mills, because you're perfect how you are."

"Ha."

Grigg paused before whatever he was going to eat next. "I'm serious, and even if you gained a hundred extra pounds, I still think you'd look sexy."

Amelia's brows pulled together, and she didn't look convinced.

"You don't think I'm serious?" Grigg challenged.

She shook her head, and Grigg rose to his feet and moved over to where she was sitting. Then he bent over and whispered something in her ear that did make her blush.

"All right, that's enough," she said with a laugh, pushing on his chest.

He returned to his chair with a satisfied look.

Amelia was far from immune to him, and he just hoped she wouldn't kick him out of her life. Not for one moment.

17

Grigg wasn't sure what he had expected when he met Amelia's mother, but it wasn't the woman standing before them in the library. Poppy wore a dress that was tighter than Silvia's had been at their dinner date and revealed more than Silvia's dress had—but Silvia was in her twenties, and Poppy had to be at least sixty. Plus, it was only about two in the afternoon. He wondered why Poppy had dressed like she was going to a red-carpet event, then he guessed that she had yet to go to bed.

It was clear that Poppy Ambrose had been doing everything possible to hide her age, including dyed hair, fake eyelashes, and whatever injections gave her outsized cheekbones and huge lips.

"Nice to meet you, Grigg," Poppy said, her smile huge—one that some men might consider dazzling.

Not Grigg. Even if he hadn't known about the way this woman had betrayed her daughter, he knew that he'd still be uncomfortable around her. Poppy extended a slender hand with long, manicured nails.

Grigg stepped forward and shook the woman's hand, then he moved back to Amelia's side.

Next Poppy turned to Amelia and held out her arms as if to hug her. But Amelia didn't react. So there was no hug or kiss between the mother and daughter. Grigg didn't blame her, not after hearing the story of her childhood and how her mother had told her significant lies.

"Imagine my surprise when Granny told me that you were here, Millie, with a *man*." Poppy's blue eyes widened to a comical effect that was more garish than anything.

"Don't call me Millie," Amelia said in a cool tone.

Grigg cut her a glance. She was staring right at her mother, no real expression on her face. He'd never seen Amelia look so . . . empty.

"Well, *I'm* your mother, and I can call you whatever I want," Poppy said in a cheerful tone that wasn't cheerful at all.

"You might have given birth to me, but you have never been a true mother to me," Amelia said, her tone still quiet, cold. "I'd appreciate it if you'd wrap up whatever business you came for, then leave. I've made plans to stay here a few days."

Poppy folded her tan-orange arms. "You don't own this house, and you can't tell me when I can or cannot stay here."

"But I can," an elderly voice said from the doorway of the library. Mrs. Lillian Ambrose entered the room in all her state. Mrs. B followed close behind, but it appeared that Lillian didn't need the extra help. Her sturdy cane was help enough. So Mrs. B murmured something about going to the kitchen and left the library.

"Mother," Poppy said in a sickly sweet tone. "You look beautiful."

The Ambrose matriarch was elegantly dressed in a white-chiffon pantsuit, but Grigg suspected Poppy's compliment was far from sincere.

Poppy reached her mother and kissed both of the woman's cheeks. "You look younger every time I see you."

"Hogwash," Lillian said, a glint of annoyance in her eyes. "What are you doing here, Poppy? I've nothing to say to you after the last time you came and demanded ridiculous things."

Grigg swallowed. He should probably go. He'd done what Amelia asked him to—come to the library with her to meet her mom—but now he was just in the way.

He bent toward Amelia. "I'll wait outside, or somewhere. This is family business."

But Amelia grasped his hand and squeezed hard. "Stay with me. Please."

Grigg was surprised, but he wasn't about to ditch Amelia if she didn't want him gone. So he remained and was gratified when she continued holding his hand.

"I have a lawyer, Mother." Poppy laughed. "You didn't think I was that smart, did you? I'll have you know that my lawyer says that your new will is, uh, how would you put it? Hogwash?"

Lillian's blue eyes blazed. "What did you do?"

Poppy clasped her long fingers together. "Nothing yet. I came to mend things between us. Extend the olive branch. You know, be a loving mother and daughter, like other people are. I am your only living child, you know."

Lillian's face drained of color.

Grigg moved into action and reached the elderly woman's side. He grasped her arm, prepared for her to faint. What Poppy had said had upset the woman enough to make her lose color completely.

Lillian rested a trembling hand over Grigg's supportive one. "You, Poppy Ambrose, are no longer welcome at Ambrose. Take your lies and your greed, and leave. I hope that I'll go to my grave without having to ever see you again."

Surprisingly, it was Amelia who spoke next. "Gran, I think we all need to calm down." She reached her grandmother too, and together, she and Grigg helped Lillian to a chair.

Then Amelia turned to Poppy. "You've upset her. I think the best thing to do is leave right now. And should you ever speak to Gran again, choose your words more carefully. You know that Sofia has power of attorney, and you can be sure that she'll hear of this."

Poppy's face went almost as pale as her mother's. Then Poppy turned and left the room, leaving no question by the rapid click of her heels that she was in a hurry.

Grigg's gaze connected with Amelia's. "Should I bring your grandmother a drink?"

Amelia nodded, but then Lillian spoke up.

"I'm fine," Lillian said. "At least I will be once Poppy is off my property. And I know that you both think I'm about to faint, but let me tell you, I would have taken her down if I weren't such a lady."

Grigg had no words. He could only stare at the Ambrose matriarch.

Then Amelia's lips twitched. Next thing he knew was that she started laughing. Lillian joined in, and Grigg was pretty sure that both women had lost their minds.

"I don't understand," Grigg said at last. "What just happened?"

"Oh, my dear," Lillian said, reaching for a tissue to wipe at her eyes, "every time Poppy and I are together, I evict her. But I've never seen her skedaddle so fast. It was rather entertaining."

Grigg caught Amelia's eye for more understanding.

"It's true," she said. "We Ambrose women are a bit hotheaded. It's that one thing I'm all right having in common with my mom."

"So you're . . . both okay?" Grigg asked.

"Maybe I will have that drink." Lillian patted Grigg's hand. "But no water for me. I'll take something a little stronger."

"Yes, ma'am." He headed out of the room and found his way to the immense kitchen. Thankfully, Mrs. B was there and was able to give him a glass of what Lillian wanted. He made his way back to the library, his mind spinning. This family of women was very complicated, and he was curious to know what the result of their verbal threats would be. Would Poppy truly sue her own mother?

When Grigg entered the library, the atmosphere was much calmer, almost peaceful.

"You're a dear man," Lillian said, accepting the glass gratefully. "Come and sit. I was just telling Amelia that Sofia found Margaret Ambrose's journal. It will explain all about the curse and how it originated." Her blue eyes twinkled. "It will also tell Amelia how to break it."

Grigg took a careful seat on the couch next to Amelia, not daring to ask questions. This moment seemed significant somehow, and he didn't know what Amelia was thinking right now. She stayed quiet, her gaze on her grandmother.

"Really, Amelia dear, you needn't be so hesitant." Lillian took a generous swallow of her drink. "Knowledge is power, you know. The more you know, the more power you'll have over your own life. And I'm pretty sure this man here is a good one and you don't want to lose him. Am I right?"

Amelia exhaled. "Why did you marry, Gran, if you knew what the curse could do? I mean, you gave us these pendants on our sixteenth birthday to protect us. What about you?"

Lillian took another sip of her drink, then she set her glass on the end table next to her chair. "I wanted you to have strength, both mentally and emotionally, against the curse. Or rumors of the curse. Whichever you believed in. I can't say that I fully believe in its power, because it's more likely the curse is only real when we *give* it power."

Amelia looked down at her clenched hands. "What about your losses, Gran?" she said in a soft voice. "Your husband and your two sons . . . ?"

Grigg frowned. This was the first he'd heard of two boys dying. Was that what Poppy had meant about being Lillian's only living child, and was that why she'd been so upset?

"I understand how you can blame my boys' deaths on a curse," Lillian said. "But they were only horrible tragedies. Nothing more."

Grigg knew that Amelia still wasn't convinced. She and her sisters had been living in fear for too many years.

"And what about Sofia's fiancé? He died in that car crash."

"Yes," Lillian agreed. "A terrible accident. It can happen to anyone." She tilted her head. "Don't let that stop you from living, Millie. Truly living."

Amelia's shoulders sagged. Grigg wanted to comfort her, but he also felt that she had to face what her grandmother was saying, because he wholeheartedly agreed.

"All right," Amelia said at last. "Where's Margaret's journal?"

Lillian smiled a gentle smile. "It's in the locked drawer of the credenza." She lifted the chain of her necklace, and Grigg saw a small key hanging from it, along with several other charms.

Amelia rose to her feet and removed the necklace from around her grandmother's neck, then crossed to the credenza. With slow movements, she unlocked the drawer, then produced a leather-bound book.

"Is this it?" Amelia asked in a soft voice.

"Yes, my dear," Lillian said. "Take your time. Read it together. And open your heart and mind to find your answers."

Amelia bit the edge of her lip and nodded. Then her gaze connected with Grigg's. "Do you mind if I read it alone first?"

"No," Grigg said automatically. He could wait, right? He'd been waiting this long. What was a little more time?

"Escort me back to my suite," Lillian told Grigg. "She'll call us when she needs us."

So Grigg did the woman's bidding. He helped her from her chair, and then he tucked her free arm into his, and together they left the library.

Mrs. B met them in Lillian's suite, and Grigg was about to leave, but Lillian said, "Stay a while. I'd like to share a few things with you.

18

THE JOURNAL AMELIA held in her hands would give her the answers she'd been so desperately searching for. At least she hoped so. And for that reason, her palms were sweating and her heart was hammering. Having her mother show up at Ambrose hadn't helped either. And now, whatever was inside these pages, Grigg would eventually know as well.

Was that good news or bad news? Could they work through this together? Could she have the confidence of her half sisters that it was truly possible to break the curse that had such power over her? Gran was right. Amelia knew it. She just had to find faith somewhere.

Amelia crossed to the chair that was closest to the empty fireplace. She used to love this spot when she was a young girl. Even with the hearth cold, it was still a cozy area. She turned the first pages and leafed through them, glancing at the handwriting of Margaret Florence Thorne Ambrose. Margaret's daughter was Helen, and Helen's daughter was Lillian.

Amelia flipped back to the first entry and read it slowly:

The Life Recordings of Margaret Florence Thorne Ambrose
Born February 9, 1874

April 23, 1893
Today I married George Frederick Ambrose II, the man I have

loved since I was sixteen years of age. In February I turned nineteen, and Father finally gave his permission. Mother wept behind her lace handkerchief like the dainty lady she has always been. Our seamstress created a perfect pink-satin gown, and George told me I looked like a princess with my long hair dressed in ringlets and jeweled combs.

It was a beautiful spring day, and after the wedding supper, we danced past midnight. Wedding guests numbered over one hundred, and the grounds were covered in buggies! All of our neighbors said it was the wedding of the decade!

Father has bestowed a most generous wedding gift upon us of three thousand pounds. George has always wanted to immigrate to America, but I shall do my best to convince him to accept Father's offer of a position at his law firm in London. I am certain that we shall be most happy!

Amelia wanted to smile at Margaret's excitement, but Amelia knew enough of family lore to realize that things didn't turn out well for Margaret. She'd lost her sons to early deaths, soon followed by her husband's death.

Amelia began to skim, turning pages faster than she could read them, looking for the events that led to the curse. Finally, she stopped on another entry that mentioned Madame Zelana, a fortune-teller who'd been commissioned to carry out the purposes of an evil woman—Mrs. Celeste Fontaine.

According to the journal entries, Margaret and Celeste Fontaine were dear friends, at least until the affair. Amelia felt sick to her stomach as she read Margaret's entry:

August 29, 1911

I have taken to my bed. I have never been so utterly and completely devastated in my entire life. Never have I wished death on someone. Especially someone that I trusted, loved, and confided in.

I have learned for myself that Mrs. Fontaine accompanied my husband—my George—to Houston to fetch Madame Zelana last

February, and they spent the night in a hotel together under a false name. The dates match up perfectly. My own friend was pregnant with my husband's child.

Celeste's baby had died, and the woman was devasted, which included making more demands on George Ambrose. Then, as if the Ambrose family weren't in enough crisis, their oldest son, Matty, had died, followed a short time later by James. Both in freak accidents.

Amelia read faster and faster. This was her family history, and it was heart-wrenching.

May 2, 1912

My hand is shaking badly as I write this, my eyes so blurry I fear I'm going blind. My limbs are weak. I have taken to my bed.

Celeste took her final revenge. Two weeks ago, after learning that George would not leave me once and for all to come to her, she cursed him so that I couldn't have him.

He died while rounding up cattle with the foreman. Kicked in the head by the sire bull, in preparation for mating season with the cows. My husband has ranched for seventeen years, and he was accompanied by experienced ranch hands no less. His accident is no coincidence.

George succumbed to death a day later after lying in a coma.

The doctor said he died of a brain hemorrhage.

In less than six months I have lost my husband and two sons. How will I ever cope—or survive out here all alone?

Amelia closed the journal with a snap.

She couldn't do it. She couldn't read any more right now. The gloom permeating from the words and sentences was a tangible thing. The room had grown chilly, and the windows dim. Was there a storm coming? She set the book on the floor and curled up on the chair, tugging the afghan from the back of the chair and wrapping up in it.

When she was seven, she'd lost her beloved father. She knew what grief and despair were. And then when she was sixteen, she'd found out the kind of person her mother really was. As much as losing her father had hurt, being betrayed by her mother had been infinitely worse.

And now, by reading the tragedy in the pages of the journal, it was like all of Amelia's wounds had been opened once again. Deep and raw.

Wind rattled the windows of the library, and moments later the rain started. Amelia loved the rain. Perhaps it was a sign. Perhaps some of the old pain could be washed away, just like the rain was now washing away the heat and dust and footprints of Ambrose.

Amelia closed her eyes against all of it. The library, the journal, the curse . . .

"Amelia?" Grigg's voice sounded far away.

She tried to open her eyes, but they were so heavy, and she was so, so tired.

Grigg said something else, but she couldn't understand him. Again her eyes wouldn't open. And then she felt herself being lifted and carried. Grigg was carrying her? Why? And where? When she felt herself placed on the softness of a bed, she wondered what time it was. But she was too tired to open her eyes and look at a clock or find out if Grigg was still with her.

The next time Amelia opened her eyes, her bedroom at Ambrose was bright with sunlight. Had the storm passed already? Had time gone backwards?

"How are you feeling?" Grigg asked, his voice a rasp.

She turned her head to see him sitting in a chair by the window. He rose, unfolded his length, and crossed to her.

He hadn't shaven, and she was surprised he could grow so many whiskers in such a short time. And he'd changed his clothing too. He wore a simple navy T-shirt and jeans. The next thing that Amelia noticed was that she was starving. Had dinner already come and gone? Why was there so much sun in her room?

"What time is it?" she managed to croak.

Grigg settled on the edge of her bed and picked up a glass of water from the side table. He helped her lift her head and take a sip. The water was cool and tasted of lemon. Signature Mrs. B.

"Thanks," Amelia murmured. "What are you doing in my bedroom?"

The edges of Grigg's mouth lifted, but she didn't miss the flash of concern in his brown eyes. "Making sure you're okay. You've been asleep for seventeen hours."

She frowned. "What?"

"I found you asleep in the library, and you wouldn't wake up," Grigg said, reaching for her hand. "Your grandmother said that you would do that when you were a little girl. Fall asleep reading in that chair. So I carried you up to bed."

"It's really the next day?"

He nodded. "I kept checking on you, but you were still asleep. I would have been worried, but your grandmother didn't seem to feel any alarm. Just said that trauma brings on exhaustion."

Amelia looked down at his hand on hers. "She's probably right."

"I'm sorry for your trauma, Mills," he said in a quiet voice. "I want to help. In any way that I can."

"I think you are helping," Amelia said. "I mean, you carried me to my bed yesterday. Is your back okay?"

He smiled. "It's okay. I'm pretty sure you could have doubled up on breakfast and I'd still be okay."

Amelia wished every moment of her life could be like these quiet ones with Grigg. "Speaking of breakfast, I'm starving."

"I thought so," Grigg said. "I'll go grab something. Wait here."

"I'll get up," she said. "Seriously. I'm not an invalid."

But Grigg leaned over and placed a firm kiss on her forehead. "Stay. Rest. I'll be right back."

So she burrowed into the covers while she waited for Grigg to return. She gazed about the room. The sunlight had turned the pale-yellow paint on the walls to a warm gold, and now the dark cherry-wood furniture gleamed. Memories of the journal entries floated through her mind, and with the passage of time, they seemed more distant—tragic still, but less potent. Almost as if Ambrose had made peace with itself.

Perhaps she could read the rest. But not alone. She wanted to be with Grigg.

She reached for her cell, then ignored any texts or missed calls and pressed SEND on Grigg's contact. He answered, "You okay?"

"I'm fine," she said with a smile. "Bring the journal up with you. I left it in the library."

He paused, then said, "Will do."

Before Grigg returned to her bedroom, Amelia had cleaned up in the bathroom and made the bed, then settled onto the loveseat near the bedroom fireplace. She scrolled through her missed calls, texts, and emails on her phone—all mostly from work. Except for the messages from Hayden. She only had to listen to one of the messages to convince her to delete them all.

Hayden was angry that she hadn't come to California. Although it sounded like he was already released and was staying at his parents. This was good news for him, right? He'd be fine, and all was well. She hoped.

She put her phone on silent, knowing she'd have to call Hayden back at some point. Just not today. Then she pulled one of the pillows close to her and hugged it against her chest.

The door cracked open, and Grigg appeared. "Feeling better?" he asked, carrying a tray and the journal into the room.

"What did you bring?"

He set the journal on the side table by the loveseat, then the tray in front of her on the small coffee table. He sat on the other end of the loveseat, giving her space. "Well, I hope you like everything. I've made an educated guess."

He'd put together a lunch tray with chicken salad, sliced cantaloupe, and juice. "I think you're looking for brownie points or something."

Grigg smiled and leaned close. "Is it working?"

"It is." She moved over and looped her arms about his neck.

Grigg's smile widened before he kissed her. Amelia closed her eyes, melting into the warmth of his touch, his embrace, and the way he kissed her ever so slowly.

His hands cradled her face, then he traced his fingers over her shoulders.

"My grandmother could walk in at any moment," Amelia finally breathed. "Remember her rule?"

"I do," Grigg whispered, trailing kisses along her neck. "She knows I brought you lunch, so we might have a little grace period."

Amelia tilted her head back as goose bumps raced along her skin. The scruff of Grigg's chin tickled her collarbone, and she laughed. Grasping the sides of his face, she lifted his head to meet her gaze. "Still. I think you need to cool things off, Mr. Edison."

His brown eyes were warm and intent on hers. "I am staying cool."

She shook her head, unable to stop her smile. "Maybe in your book, but my grandmother's an old-fashioned woman."

Grigg kissed the edge of Amelia's jaw, and for another moment, she became lost again. She couldn't believe she'd gone two years knowing this man and not enjoying everything he had to offer her.

Her stomach grumbled, and Grigg drew away with a chuckle.

"All right, eat," he said.

Amelia grinned, then reached for the tray and pulled it onto her lap. "I'll eat while you read the journal. When you catch up to where I left off, we'll read it together."

For the next hour, Amelia leaned against Grigg on the loveseat while he flipped pages in the journal. As the afternoon marched on and the sunlight deepened, the mood in the room had grown somber.

"Here." Amelia tapped the entry Grigg had just turned to. "This is where I left off. I couldn't read any more."

Grigg wrapped an arm about Amelia and pulled her closer, then kissed the top of her head. "I don't blame you. This is pretty intense stuff. I don't know how Margaret survived so much loss and betrayal."

Amelia could only nod, because her throat was feeling raw. At this moment, with Grigg's arms about her, she felt what Margaret hadn't felt most of her life. Safe and loved.

"I ache for her," Amelia said. "She's been dead for decades, yet I feel her pain as if it were my own."

"It is your own," Grigg said in a quiet voice. "There are a lot of parallels to both of your lives. Her best friend betrayed her, and you were betrayed by your mother. She lost her boys and husband at young ages. You lost your father. Twice."

Amelia nodded, her throat a lump.

"You need to know something, though," Grigg continued. "I'll never be George. What he did to his family was inexcusable, and by the time he realized his terrible mistake, it was too late."

Amelia released a shaky breath and burrowed closer to Grigg.

He tightened his hold, and she could hear his heart thumping.

"Can you read the next entry to me?" she whispered.

He hesitated. "Are you sure?"

"Yes."

He picked up the journal and turned the next page.

19

GRIGG SCANNED THE heading at the top of the next entry written by Margaret Ambrose. Her entries had morphed from that of a young woman in love to a young mother with many joys mixed with concerns, to finally, a woman who had borne difficult challenges and terrible grief. He marveled at all the woman had faced and endured, yet her legacy lived on.

Now it was time to discover whether or not Amelia and he had a future together. Because whatever was found in these pages, Amelia would have to believe she'd be able to overcome the curse.

Yesterday when Amelia had been left to read in the library, he'd spent a couple of hours listening to Lillian Ambrose's recollection of her mother, Helen. And then Lillian had told him about her daughter, Poppy.

"She's lost three of her husbands to untimely deaths," Lillian had said. "Poppy was always a self-centered child, so she gravitated toward men who would lavish her with attention. When they were taken away from her, she became desperate to control other things. Like property and money. When she comes here and makes threats, it's because she's afraid of losing someone she loves again."

Grigg supposed it made some sort of twisted sense. Poppy did things to protect herself, but that still wasn't a good enough excuse for the way she'd betrayed her own daughter. The whole situation only made Grigg feel more protective of Amelia.

He cleared his throat and began to read Margaret's words:

Life Recordings of Margaret Florence Thorne Ambrose
August 31, 1912

My brother, Lloyd, sent his dear wife across the Atlantic to be here with me for the summer. Victoria is so good, so kind. I have grown very fond of my sister-in-law. She brought her lady's maid, Nellie, with her so she wouldn't be alone on the ocean voyage.

Nellie lifts everyone's spirits with her genuine kindness and laughter and sweet singing.

Over the last few months, Victoria has tried to get me out walking in the gardens, but for most of the summer I sat on the veranda overlooking the estate in my mourning garb, just staring. Occasionally holding Helen, who is getting too big for my lap. Actually, she was too big about three years ago, but I crave her closeness, her sweetness, even when she fights to run off and swing in the gardens or play with the new kittens in the barns.

Will Celeste take her from me too? I begged Victoria to take her back to England with her to save her, but Victoria laughs off my worries. I tried to tell her about Celeste and George and the dead infant and the ties with the loss of my sons, but she is convinced it's all in my imagination.

Only I know the truth. Because I now have proof of it in Celeste's own hand.

In June, Mr. Fontaine sold their ranch and left for San Francisco with his wife. To start over and begin again.

I have never been so glad to see someone gone.

But the wicked curse that Madame Zelana concocted for my family over the last year was never undone. The fortune-teller, with her séances and mutterings from the underworld, disappeared from the village of Ambrose in June. No one knows where she went, but Celeste was sure to give me a dire warning that the Ambrose curse was in effect until someone could break it. She would not tell me how the curse was to be broken. But in July, after she and Mr. Fontaine were safely in San Francisco, I received a letter from the woman. Enclosed was the curse in Madame Zelana's own hand. Directed by Celeste for our downfall. She never could have loved George if she didn't care that he died. She only wanted me to suffer for her losses. She could not bear to know that I would have my husband and sons, and she nothing.

Since I cannot stand to look at the curse for one more second, I will write the details in my own words so my progeny will know what to do to save future generations.

Madame Zelana stated that in retribution for the loss of Celeste's son with George, and for his subsequent betrayal to her, every Ambrose son and father and brother will die. Every Ambrose daughter or woman who marries will also lose her husbands and sons. Arrogance would not save Ambrose Estate from the curse. Only George could have done that, and he had not given in to Celeste. In the end, he shunned her by not running away with her.

These facts confirmed to me—too late—that George had finally broken all association with her. Something I never believed from my husband's own mouth. Because I was too distrustful.

Celeste was bitter and vengeful. She had allowed her own sins to blacken her soul. She didn't care what her bitter envy would do to George and his family, the man she professed to love.

This is not love.

This is wickedness at its deepest depth. Madame Zelana states in her vile curse that the only way to break the hold of the curse is for every Ambrose woman to willingly give up, or lose, something they dearly love. If they do not, they too will lose the men they love. The curse was written by Madame Zelana's own hand and signed with Celeste's own blood. The devil is in the details.

I am putting this journal and Celeste's curse in my trunk of mourning clothes. Helen is too young to be told these things yet, but before she is married, I will tell her.

I have vowed to do my part. I will not return to England. I will stay here and run the ranch and estate myself. All those hours of contemplation in the gardens and ruminating on the veranda of the house George and I built together convinced me that I belong here. England holds nothing for me any longer. It has been nearly twenty years, and it would be too difficult to start over.

George worked hard for this estate with my own dowry, and it's the only way I can honor his memory and have peace within myself.

May God bless my sweet Helen and all the future generations of granddaughters so that Ambrose Estate will live on.

Be brave, Women of Ambrose Estate.

When Grigg finished, Amelia wiped at her cheeks. He reached for the tissue box and handed her a tissue.

"You okay, Mills?" he asked.

She nodded, then turned to face him on the loveseat. "It's very vague. The way to break the curse. Vague."

Grigg nodded. The words had been vague: *The only way to break the Ambrose curse is for the Ambrose women to willingly give up, or lose, something they dearly love. If they do not, they too will lose their husbands and sons.*

"It also doesn't make sense," Amelia said.

"How so?" Grigg asked.

"If you have to give up something dearly loved, wouldn't that be a child or a spouse?" She looked down at the fabric of the loveseat and ran a hand over it.

"Or the sacrifice needs to be another person or thing."

"Thing?" Amelia lifted her gaze.

"Yes, thing. Is there some *thing* you dearly love?"

"No . . ." Amelia said in a thoughtful tone. "I mean, I'm not like Sofia with her horses or Lauren with her priceless art collection. I really have no attachments."

His voice was low when he asked the next question. "Is there some*one* you love?"

Her gaze flickered from his, and his heart ached. Would she deny her feelings for him? Was he being too presumptuous to think she felt the same way about him as he did about her?

"Mills," he said in a quiet tone. "Whatever your answer is, I can take it. I told you I wanted to help you, and it's true. I want to help you. No matter what it means for me."

She was on the verge of responding when the bedroom door cracked open, and Lillian Ambrose walked into the room. At first

Grigg wondered if she'd be upset that he was in Amelia's bedroom. But her gaze was soft as she stood in the doorway, watching them.

"Gran," Amelia said. "I didn't see you there."

"You've read about the curse," Lillian said.

Amelia looked from her grandma to Grigg. "We have. And I still don't know how to break it."

Gran walked toward the loveseat, using her cane for assistance. She settled in the chair across from them, unbothered that Amelia's bedroom was the location for this discussion.

"You need to look deep inside of yourself, Millie dear," Lillian Ambrose said. "What is it that you hold close? A thing? A person? An emotion?"

20

AMELIA DIDN'T KNOW how to answer Gran's questions. Who did she hold close to her heart? Two people.

She looked at Grigg. She held him close to her heart. Not that she had admitted it yet. And Gran. Amelia held her grandmother close to her heart. Was that what the curse required? That she break up with Grigg?

"Grigg is not who you need to let go of," her grandmother said, as if she'd read Amelia's thoughts. "Breaking the curse is what will give the two of you a future together—should you choose each other, of course."

Amelia's skin warmed. She would choose him, and just now she realized how much she wanted that option. Not any of the men on her list. She hadn't even given Peter or Jack a chance, and she never would. Neither of them compared to Grigg in any way. She exhaled. "All right, Gran. What are you saying?"

Gran leaned forward, her blue eyes bright. "You have to lose the thing that is stopping you from progressing and preventing you from enjoying relationships." Her lips curved. "Let go of your anger, Millie, and forgive your mother."

Amelia didn't speak. She couldn't even move. She only stared at her grandmother. What she was asking was utterly impossible.

"It's been years since your father's death, over eight if I can still do math at my age," Gran said in a gentle voice. "By forgiving your mother, you will be freed. Freed of your anger, freed of your broken heart, and freed of this curse."

Amelia stood from the loveseat. With Grigg and Gran watching her, she paced the room. This was nothing close to what her half sisters had said they'd lost or given up. Forgiveness was not a tangible thing, was it?

After several moments, she finally turned to her audience and folded her arms. "I don't know how to do it. I don't know if it's possible."

"Come here, Millie," Gran said, holding out her hand.

Amelia crossed to her and took the thin, veined hand.

"Forgiveness is possible," Gran said. "I've lived too many years to deny it. Sometimes the first step is forgiving yourself."

Amelia's eyes widened. "What do *I* have to forgive myself for?"

Gran only smiled that knowing smile of hers. "When you start considering the possibilities, you'll discover many things to forgive yourself for. Such as your part in the deception by your mother."

Amelia frowned. "*My* part? I was seven."

"Yes," Gran agreed. "You were an innocent seven-year-old child when your father abandoned both you and your mother. She was betrayed, too, you see."

Amelia folded her arms. "It's not the same thing."

"It doesn't have to be the same thing to understand another person's hurt and fear," Gran said. "I am not saying that your mother did the right thing. Not at all. She made a terrible mistake, one that she regrets."

"Regrets?" Amelia shot out, knowing that her emotions were on the edge. "If Poppy regrets it, she sure hasn't shown it, to me or to you. She's been awful to you, Gran. How can you defend her?"

Gran merely nodded. "She has been awful. And she has also been hurt, deeply hurt. When you consider your losses and grievances, also consider hers."

Amelia turned from Gran and crossed to the bed, then perched on the edge of it. Did Grigg agree with her grandmother? "How can you say that about Poppy? The woman who calls herself a mother? She said horrible things to you just yesterday."

Gran folded her hands on top of her cane. "Those horrible words are a manifestation of her pain and regret. Some of it stems from how she treated you."

This only bothered Amelia more. "So now it's my fault that she's the way she is?"

"Oh no, that's not what I meant." Gran rose to her feet, her limbs surprisingly steady.

Grigg moved to help her, but she waved him off.

Amelia watched her grandmother walk toward her. A beautiful, stately woman who, no matter the crisis, kept a level head.

"Millie dear," Gran said when she reached Amelia's side. "This is not something to be solved with a simple conversation. It might take you days or weeks or even years to come to your solution on how forgiveness will work in your life. But I can promise you this, dear: it will be worth it in the end."

Amelia breathed in, breathed out. Deep inside her broken soul, she knew her grandmother was right. But at this moment, she couldn't fathom forgiving the woman who'd given birth to her. Amelia closed her eyes, thinking of her lost father, who was buried on the Ambrose property. Along with all the other men and boys.

If it took forgiving Poppy to end this curse, would it be worth it? Of course it would. But getting there was another matter.

Amelia opened her eyes to meet Gran's steady gaze. "I'll try," she whispered. "I can't promise anything." She looked at Grigg, and she saw both hope and sorrow in his eyes.

If anything, he knew her history with her mother, so he now knew that there was no free sailing to break the curse made so long ago.

Gran patted Amelia's hand. "You are doing the right thing, dear. I'm proud of you."

Amelia swallowed against the tightness of her throat. "Don't be proud of me yet. I don't know if I can."

Gran only nodded. Then she motioned for Grigg to help her out of the room. "I think I'll lie down for a short while," she told him as they reached the hallway.

Amelia scanned the bedroom, the beautiful furnishings, the soft, warm colors. How did Gran do it? How had she managed so many family dynamics for so many years, yet extended compassion again and again to the one person who should be the most loyal—her own daughter?

Amelia found her shoes and pulled them on. Then she grabbed a ponytail holder and wrapped her hair into a messy bun. She needed to get out of the house. Walk as far as she could. Find the answers within herself.

Just as she reached the top of the stairs to head to the main floor, Grigg came along the upper hallway.

His eyes widened when he saw her. "Are you leaving?"

"Just for a walk," she said, but she didn't miss the relief in his eyes.

He nodded. "Want some company?"

"No." She knew he was disappointed, but she had a lot to think over without his presence to distract her. So she walked toward him, placed her hands on his forearms, then lifted herself up on her toes to kiss him softly. "Thank you for taking care of me today. And last night. And pretty much all the time."

His lips curved. "My pleasure."

"I'll be an hour or two," she said. "And I have my cell."

"Okay." He ran his fingers across her cheek, then down her neck. "Be safe."

She nodded, then stepped back. Her heart hitched at the way Grigg stood there watching her. As if he was going to miss her or something.

But Amelia was determined to clear her mind. Everything seemed dependent on the next actions she took, and she had to think through them carefully. Once out of the house, she walked slowly through the back garden. She turned her phone on in case Grigg or Gran needed to get a hold of her.

Then she decided to call Hayden and get things over with once and for all.

He answered on the second ring. "Are you on your way?" he asked without any other preamble.

"On my way where?" she asked, her stomach already knotting.

"To my place," he said. "Didn't you get my message? I flew back to Denver this morning. The doctors say that I need to take it easy for about a week, so I need you to help me out—"

"I'm in Texas," Amelia said quickly, cutting him off. "I told you I had a family emergency."

"Oh, at your grandma's? Did she die or something?"

"No," Amelia said.

Hayden's entire tone changed from put out to curious. "Is she still running that place?"

Amelia exhaled. "She is."

"How is she doing?"

Amelia's heart softened just a tad. She'd nearly reached the end of the garden path, and she paused in a shady spot. "She's very well. I think she'll outlast us all."

Hayden laughed. "You may be right."

She smiled, but Hayden's next comment made her smile drop.

"When can you be here?" he asked. "I mean, if everything's fine with your grandma, then return to Denver to help me out."

Here it was. The chance to come clean with Hayden. "I don't think that's such a good idea. I need to tell you something, Hayden."

"Why do I get the feeling you're about to dump me again?" His voice was hard, edgy, not that she blamed him.

Amelia wanted to backtrack, and she definitely didn't want to bring Grigg into the middle of it. After all, he had been at their double date. "Over this past week, I realized that I need to take a step back from everything." This was mostly true, right? "So many things have changed recently in my life, and I need to take the time to let those things settle."

"What are you talking about?" Hayden asked, his tone definitely upset. "*You* called *me*. *You* asked me out."

Amelia began to walk again, leaving the garden and walking toward the cemetery the long way. "I know, and I'm glad we got together. For what it's worth, it was good seeing you again. I just . . . I wanted to see you so that I could find out if there was anything between us still."

Hayden's laugh was bitter. "And now that I need you, need some help, you're copping out on me."

"It's not like that," Amelia protested.

"You're a piece of work, Amelia Ambrose," Hayden spat out. "You're a tease, you know that, and that's about the worst thing a woman can be."

Anger and guilt battled it out in Amelia's heart. She *had* called him. She had given him hope. But still. "I didn't mean to lead you on, Hayden," she said. "It was one date, though. A casual date at that. I don't think I'm a criminal for asking you out and then not wanting to continue to see you."

Hayden didn't speak for so long that Amelia wondered if he'd hung up. But when she checked her phone, the line was still active. "Hayden?"

"I'm not going to let you get away with this," he said at last, his tone cold.

"What are you talking about?" A slow chill had crept up her spine, and her mind raced. Was Hayden threatening her? Or was he just saying stupid stuff because he was upset? Or maybe he was on some sort of painkiller?

He didn't answer. This time the line went completely silent. He'd hung up.

Even though the sun was warm overhead, the chill remained as Amelia continued toward the cemetery. She didn't know how to read into Hayden's comment. She didn't think he was dangerous or violent or a stalker or anything. Well, maybe he'd been a little obsessive last time they'd called things off. He had kept reaching out to her for a couple of weeks.

It wasn't like their paths would naturally cross anyway. He'd have to deliberately seek her out to see her. And that gave Amelia a little comfort, because she didn't think Hayden would go that far. Besides, he was a university professor. Well educated, successful in his field, intelligent. He was just in a rough patch.

Amelia pocketed her phone and continued into the graveyard. She walked among the headstones, thinking about what Gran had counseled her to do. Was that really the answer? Forgiving Poppy?

Amelia didn't see how it was possible. Could she just say, "I forgive you," to Poppy and be done with it? No. Of course not.

She walked to her father's headstone. As the trees whispered above her and the breeze stirred the grass at her feet, she wondered what her dad's opinion was in all of this. Why had he left Poppy in the first place? Okay, so maybe Amelia could deduce that reason. Marrying a woman with three children already would have been a difficult life.

But why had her father left *his* little girl? He'd sent her letters—this she found out later, after the Great Confrontation. Amelia still had the letters from her dad, written simply to the seven-year-old girl that she was at the time.

Since she never wrote him back, thinking he was dead, the letters had stopped after a few months. What had her dad thought of her?

Amelia sat cross-legged in front of the headstone and picked at the cool blades of grass. Rubbing them between her fingers, she thought of her dad's feelings. Something she hadn't considered before. Yes, he'd left a bad marriage, but his own daughter hadn't ever responded to his letters. Granted, Amelia was seven, but she'd been a good writer and reader even at that age.

"I didn't abandon you, Dad," Amelia whispered to the headstone bearing her father's name. Tears pricked her eyes. "Mom betrayed us both. First she drove you off, then she kept us apart. Forever."

The words stuck in her throat, and Amelia closed her eyes. The first step in the entire situation had been her father deciding to leave. The next step had been her father relying on letters—between himself and a seven-year-old. How reliable had he expected that to be? He knew she was alive. *He* could have come to visit. Made more of an effort. *He* was the adult with the car and resources.

Amelia pulled her knees against her chest and exhaled. Perhaps forgiving Poppy started with forgiving her father.

21

SQUARE ONE WAS not where Grigg had expected to be when he returned to Denver. He also hadn't expected to return alone. But that was what had happened. Amelia said she needed another day at Ambrose, alone. Grigg hadn't needed more explanation to understand that she wanted a break from him.

Walking out of the airport alone and taking the shuttle to where he'd parked the car made him feel like he'd forgotten something. Or someone, more accurately. Back in Texas. He hated that Amelia was still so hurt over her mother's actions, and after meeting Poppy, Grigg could honestly say that he despised the woman too.

But Gran's statements had made sense as well. Even if there was no Ambrose curse to contend with, carrying so much pain and trauma for so many years would never let Amelia progress in her relationships. And Grigg sure hoped that he would be part of that progression.

After finding his SUV in the parking lot, he unlocked it. He slid into the front seat, again, alone. Doubts plagued him as he checked his phone for any missed calls or texts. Nothing. Just like there'd been nothing when the plane landed.

Grigg didn't like Amelia going silent. Not at all. Even if they weren't in this complicated relationship of theirs, there should still be business matters to discuss, right? There were always business matters.

Yet Grigg drove to the office in the light midmorning traffic with no idea of what Amelia was thinking or doing right now. *Call me,* he drummed onto the steering wheel. *Come back to Denver.*

He'd be patient. It was all he could do, and what he'd been doing for a long time anyway. What was a few more hours, days? Even weeks. Hell, he'd wait years if he knew there was hope at the end of it all. And if there was no guarantee? He'd still make a fool of himself over Amelia Ambrose. Because no matter how much he tried to talk himself out of loving a woman who had no power over her own destiny, he knew he wanted to be with her every step of the way. Whichever direction that took.

"You're back," Silvia said as he walked into the main lobby.

He was surprised to see her working the morning shift. Her typical hours were evening, and he usually saw her when he was leaving the building.

"I'm back," Grigg said, slowing his step to be polite. "How's everything?"

Silvia shrugged, and a small pout graced her red-painted lips. "Boring."

He knew this was a segue for him to stop and flirt, but he wasn't interested. And never had been, he realized.

"Maybe download the Kindle app to your phone and read a book?" He knew the statement was petty, but he didn't care.

Silvia's eyes narrowed, and he could swear she threw an invisible knife at his back while he waited at the elevator bank. Once he was inside the elevator, his cell rang. His heart betrayed him and was pounding by the time he'd retrieved the phone from his pocket.

He didn't recognize the number, though. Would Amelia be calling from another phone? So Grigg answered.

"Hey, buddy," the man said on the other end of the line.

"Hey," Grigg said.

"Back in town already?"

Grigg frowned. "Yep. Who's this?"

The man chuckled. "Of course you'd ask that. Too much of a hotshot to have my little ole number in your contacts?"

The elevator doors slid open, and Grigg stepped out onto the floor. Across from the elevators, a glass door read *Ambrose & Edison*

Investment Firm. He paused outside the door, not wanting to take the conversation into the reception area.

"Who's calling?" Grigg asked, his patience almost out.

The man laughed again. "Hayden. You know, the guy Amelia dumped?"

This, Grigg didn't know . . . well, at least not in those exact terms. He'd assumed Amelia had blown Hayden off, but this all sounded pretty official.

"I'll bet you're pretty happy about it too," Hayden continued. "Since you're getting the goods now."

"Did you seriously refer to Amelia as 'the goods'?" Grigg gripped the phone tighter. Who did this guy think he was? They'd gone on a double date, and it wasn't anything to become this possessive over.

Hayden lowered his voice to a whisper. "She was mine before she was yours, sir."

"You piece of sh—"

The call ended, and Grigg was left fuming, holding a dead phone in his hand.

He didn't move for a moment, too stunned by what had happened. Hayden was downright creepy, and Grigg had the sudden feeling he needed to warn Amelia. About what, exactly, he wasn't sure yet. He called her number, but she didn't answer. So he texted her: *Had a strange phone call with Hayden. Don't answer any of his calls.*

Then Grigg headed into his office, greeting a couple of people as he went, but as soon as he could, he shut his office door. Sitting in the chair behind his desk, he began to google Hayden Black, checking for anything on social media that the guy might have posted.

But there was nothing recent and nothing that raised red flags.

When a text buzzed his phone, Grigg snatched it from the top of the desk. Not from Amelia.

It was from Hayden.

Watch your back, buddy.

Now, what did that mean? Grigg screenshotted the text, then saved it to a new album on his phone. If Hayden thought this was funny, he would think twice.

The rest of the day dragged as Grigg caught up on work and

waited for any response from Amelia. So far, she hadn't replied to his text, although he could see that she'd read the thing. Finally, in the afternoon, he broke down and called her again.

She answered on the second ring, out of breath. "Hi, I just got to the airport."

"You're coming home?" he asked. *Home* being a relative word.

"I am," she said. "And I think I have good news."

Grigg realized he was grinning, his relief was so great. "What is it?"

Her laugh was soft. "You'll find out. Pick me up?"

Grigg was already standing. "Of course. What time do you fly in?"

"About six thirty p.m."

He nodded even though she couldn't see him. Any other work tasks were a wash today, and Grigg closed his laptop and slipped it into his computer bag. "Great. I'll be there."

He heard the sound of an announcer in the airport in the background.

"Can't wait to see you," she said.

Grigg's heart thumped, and he wasn't sure how he'd make it waiting for the next few hours.

"Gotta go," she said. "We're boarding."

She hung up before Grigg had a chance to reply. And before he had a chance to warn her again about Hayden. No matter. There would be time for that. He left the office, whistling as he went.

He'd go home for a bit, get cleaned up, and then head to the airport. If there was ever a time that afternoon traffic in Denver didn't bother him, this was it. He wasn't in a huge rush, since he had plenty of time. Although the faster the time passed, the better. He'd pick up Boomer from Spencer's later that night.

Grigg wondered if Amelia had talked to her grandmother about everything again. Had Amelia gone so far as to call Poppy or even meet with her? Was that why she was so excited to talk to him? They'd finally made peace, and now . . . life could move forward for all of them?

Perhaps Grigg should have been on alert, but nothing piqued his senses when he unlocked his condo door and strode into the cool, dim interior. He set his keys on the kitchen table and moved to open the fridge to fetch a cold water bottle, when something in his peripheral vision moved. A tall form.

Grigg spun around, confused and surprised all at once, when the man swung a heavy object against the side of his face. The only extreme pain Grigg had to compare the blow to was when he'd blown his ACL playing football.

This hurt more. He toppled to the ground, and somehow his limbs didn't work in helping him get back on his feet. The man stood over him, the object raised again.

"Hayden," Grigg mouthed. But the name was silent on his tongue. Because the man brought the object down on Grigg's head again.

This time he didn't try to get up. He didn't know how long he lay prostrate on the floor, blacked out, but the next time he opened his eyes, he tasted blood in his mouth.

Grigg groaned as the memory of Hayden attacking him came rushing back to his mind.

Why had Hayden come over? The man was crazy, there was no doubt, but even a crazy action had a motivation behind it. And Grigg, though his head was throbbing and his pulse pounding, could think of only one motivation.

Amelia.

Slowly, Grigg rolled over onto his side and began to move various parts of his body. Nothing was broken, unless one counted that he likely had a concussion. He sat up, moving as gently as he could, and all the while his pulse skyrocketed with anger. Hayden wouldn't get away with this.

Once on his feet, Grigg held onto the back of a kitchen chair for several moments, waiting for the dizziness to pass. He couldn't see his phone anywhere, and it wasn't in his pocket. Had he left it in the car? Then his gaze landed on the clock above the microwave. It was already after 6:30 p.m. How long had he been out?

He had to get ahold of Amelia. She might be at the curb right at that moment, trying to contact him. He'd somehow make it to the SUV, grab his phone, and get ahold of Amelia. But where had his car keys gone? Not on the table. Had he left them somewhere else before Hayden struck?

Grigg lifted a hand to the side of his face, pressing against the tenderness there as he tried to think what he'd done with his keys. Had he left them in the car too?

Possibly. He walked out of the kitchen, taking slow, measured steps. His head still throbbed, and his stomach twisted with nausea. In the entryway, he caught his reflection in the hall mirror. Hayden had got him good.

There was a bump on his temple, and there were scratches down the side of his face. Grigg released a hiss, then opened the front door and stepped onto the stoop. The place he'd parked his car ninety minutes ago was empty. Grigg looked left, then right. No SUV in sight. That was impossible, of course. Maybe he'd parked farther away? But that didn't make sense. He had an assigned spot, and that's where he'd always parked. For two years.

Grigg's breath shortened, and he leaned against the doorframe for support. His phone, his keys, and his SUV were all gone. The coincidence was too great.

Hayden had gone to pick up Amelia.

A few months ago, Grigg had canceled the landline that came with the condo. So he had no backup phone. He walked over to the next door neighbor's, but no one answered his knock. He continued to the office and freaked out the woman working at the desk. Brandy quickly handed him the phone, and the first call he made was to Amelia's cell. Thankfully he had it memorized. She didn't answer, so he left a message.

Then he called again. Still no answer.

Next he called Ambrose Estate.

William Shelton, the chauffeur, answered the call. When Grigg told Shelton about his worry about Hayden, the man promised to keep trying to get ahold of Amelia. Grigg hung up with Shelton, and turned to the office worker. "Can I use your cell phone and car?"

Brandy's eyes bugged out.

"Please," Grigg said. "It's an emergency. See what this guy did to me. He'll do worse to my girlfriend." Grigg wasn't sure if *girlfriend* was the right word for Amelia, but he had to convince Brandy to help him out.

"Okay," Brandy said, then handed over her phone and keys. "It's the black Nissan."

"Thanks." Grigg headed toward the door. His head was swimming, and he probably shouldn't drive, but he couldn't sit around either.

On the way he called the police and explained things as best as he could. But by the time he arrived at the airport, there was no sign of Amelia or his car.

22

AMELIA WAVED DOWN Grigg's SUV the moment she saw it round the bend of the pickup lane. The sun had just set, but beyond the headlights, she recognized the vehicle. She couldn't wait to see him and tell him about her decisions. She'd spent hours sitting at her father's grave earlier that day, just like the day before, and she'd come to several realizations.

First, that she had already forgiven her father. Yes, both her parents had been responsible in different ways for how things played out, but her father had taken the more permanent step. Then her mother had reacted to that step, in utterly the wrong way—but Amelia knew she personally had to start with her father.

After the time spent sitting next to her father's headstone, she'd spent another couple of hours with Gran. They'd talked through everything in detail. They'd cried, and they'd even laughed some, while Gran told Amelia about her dad. Much of it Amelia had forgotten.

But then a truly remarkable thing had happened. Amelia had felt the presence of her father in Gran's suite of rooms. Amelia couldn't quite explain it, but she knew he was there, listening, perhaps even crying and laughing along with them. At one point, Amelia turned from Gran and spoke into the air. "Hi, Daddy. I love you, and I want you to know I forgive you."

The words were simple, but spoken aloud, they somehow carried power.

Gran had only smiled and wiped away her own tears.

So . . . this gave Amelia confidence that she could move onto the next step. The harder step, but the most necessary. Forgive Poppy.

And she wanted Grigg with her when she went to visit her mother. That might prove a schematic challenge, but Amelia was up for it. A new beginning with Grigg was more important than holding onto her anger against her mother.

The SUV slowed, and Amelia couldn't hold back a grin. Grigg had better be prepared to accept a giant hug and maybe entertain a little kissing.

But the man who climbed out of Grigg's vehicle wasn't Grigg at all.

"Hayden," Amelia said, too shocked to wrap her mind around why he'd be driving Grigg's SUV.

Hayden gave her a half smile and strode to her. He wasn't wearing his usual button-down shirt, worn khakis, and bow tie. Instead, he wore sweats and a T-shirt. It was probably what he was convalescing in.

Amelia took a step back, toward the middle of the sidewalk. "What are you doing here?"

"Long story, but Grigg's hurt," Hayden said. "He called me to come get you."

"He's hurt?"

"There was a break-in at his place," Hayden said. "He's getting checked out at the hospital, but I'm sure he'll be okay."

A dozen thoughts and emotions collided within Amelia's mind. If Grigg was in the hospital, did that mean it was hopeless to break the curse? A well of panic began in her chest, spreading to her tightening throat.

"Come on," Hayden said. "I'll take you straight to the hospital to see him."

Her mind was still trying to catch up. "You drove his SUV?" Amelia looked from Hayden to the SUV.

"I was almost out of gas, and I didn't want to take the time to stop, so Grigg told me to take his," Hayden said. "I'm the one who dropped him off at the hospital. He was just going to sit home with an ice bag on his face."

"His face?" she echoed.

"Yeah, got clocked pretty good." Hayden stepped to the passenger door and opened it. "Come on, Grigg will be asking for you. Can't leave your business partner hanging."

Everything inside her screamed not to get into the SUV with Hayden, but what other choice did she have? Her cell phone was dead, and at least she could charge it up in the SUV. She'd probably see missed calls and texts from Grigg explaining that Hayden was coming to pick her up. After all, she hadn't told Grigg about her most recent bothersome conversation with Hayden.

So Amelia climbed into the passenger seat and clipped on her seatbelt. Hayden put her luggage in the back of the SUV, then came around to the driver's side.

He flashed her a smile, then pulled away from the curb.

"Where's the USB cord?" Amelia asked.

"The what . . . ?"

Amelia searched around the front of the SUV, opening the glove box, then feeling underneath the seat. Then she turned and saw the edge of it peeking out from beneath the floor mat between the two sets of seats. "That's weird," she said, then pulled it out.

She turned forward again and plugged the USB cord into the outlet, then attached her phone.

"You won't be needing that," Hayden said.

"My phone's dead," Amelia said. "I want to see how Grigg's doing."

Then she watched in astonishment as Hayden unplugged her phone, then tossed it out the window onto the dark road.

She grabbed his arm as she realized what he was doing, but it was too late. "What did you do? Stop the car!"

Hayden merely returned both hands to the wheel and drove.

"Turn around," Amelia said. "You threw my phone out the window. How could you do that?" She reached for her door handle and tugged. She didn't really intend to open the door and jump out or anything, but she was surprised to find it locked. And it couldn't be unlocked. Hayden had the safety locks engaged.

Then her mind caught up with the events of the past few moments. Hayden picking her up at the airport. Hayden throwing her phone out the window. Hayden locking the safety locks.

Her stomach roiled. Hayden had turned into someone she didn't know, someone whom perhaps she'd never known. It was then she realized they weren't headed into town. They were driving in the opposite direction, away from the city and the airport.

"Stop the car," she said. "Right now!"

Hayden only sped up. "Keep quiet, sweetheart, or you'll regret it."

The mildness of his voice was more creepy than yelling. She glanced around the SUV, wondering if he had a gun or another weapon. The thought made her shudder. A man's bare hands could be equally lethal. Hayden had a good fifty or sixty pounds on her, and he was definitely stronger than she was.

Breathe, Amelia, breathe, she silently commanded herself.

There weren't many cars on this stretch of road, but Amelia would find someone to help her, somehow. The sun had fully set, and twilight had dissipated into the inky black of the moonlit sky. She could escape the car and find somewhere to hide. Yanking the wheel would only hurt the both of them, and she didn't know if she could temporarily disable him while driving. They'd probably wreck, and then could she still get away from him if she was injured? Her panicked mind raced through a dozen more possibilities.

Maybe when they reached wherever he was driving, she could escape then. Without a cell phone she'd have to do a good job of outrunning him before she could find some help.

Making as little movement as possible, she slipped off her heels, keeping her gaze forward. She focused on the passing scenery, trying to gauge where they were going and what his plans might be. She chanced speaking again. "Is Grigg really in the hospital?"

Hayden scoffed. "Nah. Although I did get him pretty good. He'll be sore for a while."

Amelia's eyes popped wide. "What did you do to him?"

"We had a little scuffle," he said with a shrug, then he met her gaze with a smile.

The smile felt like a knife to her heart.

"I don't think you should be worrying about Grigg right now," Hayden said. "I've got other plans for you."

Amelia swallowed against the lump in her throat, but she didn't look away from the man. "What kind of plans?"

"You'll see, sweetheart," Hayden said. "Now keep quiet."

Her eyes burned, and she wanted to throw up. The passing scenery told her they were getting more and more remote. Then suddenly Hayden veered to the side of the road and cut through some underbrush. The SUV bumped along until he stopped near a copse of trees.

Was this it? His planned destination?

"Get down," Hayden hissed, shutting off the SUV and turning off the lights.

Amelia only obeyed because he'd latched onto her arm, bruising where his fingers dug into her skin. Hayden's breathing was rapid, matching her own heartbeat, but she held her breath, wondering what he was hiding from.

And then the dimness of the SUV was cut by flashes of lights—red and blue.

Amelia raised her head. Two cop cars were passing by on the road, driving slowly. Hayden grabbed her hair and yanked her back down. Amelia cried out, and he slapped a hand over her mouth.

"Shut up, woman!" he hissed.

Amelia couldn't let this happen. If Hayden had a gun, wouldn't he have already pulled it on her? And if she let the cops pass, then would she have another opportunity to get away?

But then again, if Hayden did have a gun, she wouldn't get very far.

Her heart screamed to run, while the pain in her scalp from Hayden's grip told her to obey.

Amelia squeezed her eyes shut, thinking of what her female relatives might do in this situation. Gran. Poppy. Margaret Ambrose.

Margaret had let her husband and a woman named Celeste Fontaine run roughshod over her, and look at the suffering Margaret had endured her entire life. A husband and two sons lost to her forever. She'd let someone else determine her fate.

Amelia didn't want that for herself. She didn't want anyone, especially Hayden, to hold her back from living her life. To stop her dreams.

She took a deep breath, then turned her head enough so that she could bite down on Hayden's arm.

"Damn you!" he spat, and for a split second, he relaxed his grip on her hair.

But Amelia only needed that split second.

She pushed herself across his lap by using her feet against her door as leverage. Unlocking the car, she then drove her head back, connecting the back of her head with Hayden's face. This time he cried out in pain, but his arms snaked around her. Amelia was ready. She elbowed him in the gut as hard as she could, then she opened the door and scrambled out of the car.

Her ankle twisted beneath her as she landed on the ground in her haste, but she didn't care about the pain. She had a cop car to alert. Running, she headed toward the road, her feet slipping more than once in the rocks and dirt. Her breathing came in great gulps, but she was able to muster enough voice to scream. "Stop! I'm here! Wait!"

When she reached the road, the fading lights of the two cop cars told her they were at least a half mile away. She started to run after them, tears coursing down her cheeks, her pounding footsteps on the pavement echoing like a shot through her entire body. She didn't know how much longer her ankle would hold out, but that could be attended to much later.

The moonlight gave her enough light to see the road by, but the trees and scattered bushes of what lay beyond the road were only murky shapes. If she left the road, could she truly find a place to hide? Or would Hayden simply follow her trail? Then, above her footsteps and her own breathing, she heard Hayden running after her. He was making small grunts as if he were an Olympic athlete throwing a javelin. Cold rushed through Amelia's veins. She'd have to hide somewhere after all.

Scanning desperately for a place she could lose Hayden, she felt her ankle pop. The pain lanced through her, and she almost tripped and fell. She couldn't stop. She couldn't slow down. She had to keep moving as fast as she could. But even as she pushed herself harder and harder, her steps were slowing down and Hayden was gaining on her.

23

G**RIGG HAD NEVER** been so sick to his stomach in his life. Not even the moment when he knew he'd torn the tendons in his knee and effectively ruined his football career in one lousy play. Amelia was out there, somewhere, with the bastard Hayden. And Grigg was going to find him and make him wish he'd never set eyes on Amelia Ambrose.

Grigg had followed the cop cars in Brandy's car, and he was grateful the little vehicle had some sporty spunk. He probably shouldn't be speeding after racing cop cars, but he wasn't going to leave the search for Amelia to chance. Thankfully, the cops had been able to activate the GPS tracker on his SUV, and they'd located the vehicle about ten miles from the airport.

Bypassing the airport altogether, Grigg headed in the same direction as Hayden. But now the cop cars were slowing down, so Grigg did too. Had they spotted the SUV? Was Hayden up ahead?

Grigg slowed even more, giving at least a mile's distance between him and the cops. He'd let them do their work, but if they came upon the SUV, he wanted to be there. Come what may. If Amelia needed defending, then Grigg would be there in the middle of it. He had no problem inserting himself. So what if his head throbbed and his eye was half swollen now? He was no stranger to pain.

The cop cars continued their slow speed, and Grigg kept his distance, scanning the road and the terrain beyond as he drove. Another car came toward him from the other direction, and Grigg slowed down even more. It wasn't an SUV, and he released a breath as it passed.

Then, several hundred yards up ahead, he saw a person run out onto the road. Well, he was limping and running. Grigg's heart nearly stopped. Was it Hayden? No . . . the person was too small.

Amelia!

He simply stared for a moment. She was running toward the cop cars. Grigg sped up, putting on his flashers, hoping that would signal he was there to help her. Then another form emerged onto the road. There was no doubt this larger person was Hayden. And he wasn't limping, and he was plainly moving faster than Amelia. Which meant he'd catch her soon.

Grigg began to honk, hoping to deter Hayden, make him slow down, distract him, anything.

Hayden did look behind him, but he only moved to the side of the road and kept running.

Amelia had also moved to the side, and Grigg stepped on the accelerator, pulling ahead of Hayden. Then in a single movement, he slammed on his brakes and jerked the wheel so that the car spun in front of Hayden. Before the car came to a complete stop, Grigg opened his door and jumped out of the car.

Hayden veered off the road, now running in an arc to avoid Grigg and his car.

"Drop to the ground!" Grigg called out, even though he didn't have any sort of weapon to back up his threat.

Hayden hesitated just enough to give Grigg an added advantage.

"Grigg!" a woman screamed.

But he didn't answer. His sole focus was the man who'd just turned coward and was now making a beeline for the trees beyond. Grigg might have given up running long distances due to his knee injury, but he hadn't slacked off of staying in shape. When Hayden reached a tangle of bushes, Grigg plowed into him from behind.

The two of them tumbled to the ground.

Hayden yelled curses and fought like a cornered cat, but Grigg wasn't about to be blindsided again.

Grigg pinned Hayden to the ground, shoving his knee against the man's throat until he was gasping for air. Grigg held down Hayden's wrists, using all his strength to keep the man from lashing out.

"Grigg!" Amelia cried out, closer now.

"Stay back!" Grigg said without turning. "Keep on the road and signal the cops if they turn around." He hoped his honking and flashers had drawn their attention.

Hayden jerked and twisted beneath him, and Grigg got a good look at the whites of the man's eyes in the moonlight.

"You're done, man," Grigg spat out.

"Let me go," Hayden ground out, his mouth sounding like it was full of marbles as Grigg kept the pressure on his neck.

"They're coming," Amelia called, her voice farther away.

"It must be your lucky day," Grigg told Hayden. "Because if it were up to me, you wouldn't live to see your day in court."

Hayden's eyes rolled back, and Grigg knew the man had only passed out. And that he should release him. But the adrenaline pumping through his body was hard to calm down.

"Hands up!" a voice barked.

The cops.

Grigg eased his knee from Hayden's throat, then slowly stood. "I got him," he said, raising his own hands as he turned to face the three cops approaching the scene.

Behind them, Amelia released a choked sob.

Grigg stepped away from the prone Hayden, and two of the cops moved forward. One of them cuffed the unconscious man.

"He'll be awake soon enough," Grigg said, his hands still raised. "I'm Grigg Edison. The one who called in the alert."

The third cop nodded and said, "You can stand down, but I want to see your ID."

Grigg lowered his hands, then fished his wallet out of his pocket and showed his ID to the cop. He could hear Amelia crying quietly, and as soon as the cop cleared him, he walked over to her.

"Mills," he said as he approached her. "Are you hurt?"

She melted into his arms, and he pulled her close. "I'm okay. What about you? I was so worried. Hayden said . . . he said that you were injured."

He closed his eyes and tightened his hold. "Hayden attacked me, but it's nothing. Nothing compared to what you've gone through." He drew away and gazed into her eyes. "Your ankle is hurt. What else?"

She wiped at the tears on her cheeks. "Just my ankle. He only . . . he only scared me."

Grigg drew her close again. The anger inside simmered, and it was a good thing that the cops had secured Hayden in the back of their car, because Grigg would like nothing more than to punch him out.

"We need to get you checked out at the hospital," Grigg said. "And the cops are going to want a report as well. Are you up for it?"

She nodded against his chest, keeping her arms tight about him. Sure enough, one of the cops approached, and after several questions, Grigg told the cop to follow them to the hospital. Amelia could answer the rest of the questions there.

The next few hours were grueling, but at least Grigg had Amelia back. The X-ray tech at the hospital reported nothing had been broken, just sprained. While her ankle was being iced, Amelia told the cop everything that had happened, including the phone calls they'd shared leading up to tonight.

Grigg kept her hand clasped in his, and he marveled at her courage. She'd jumped out of the SUV and started running after the cops, Hayden right behind her. Thankfully, Hayden hadn't had a gun, or things could have been much, much different.

By midnight, everything had wound down, and Grigg was able to find out from the cop that Hayden had been booked into jail with no chance of bail. This set his mind at ease for the time being.

"Ready?" Grigg asked Amelia after the attending doctor cleared them to leave.

She met his gaze, her blue eyes a well of trust in him. "I'm ready."

"Why don't you come to my place?" he said. "You can sleep in my room, and I'll take the couch."

"I don't want to put you out," she said.

"I insist," he said. "It will help me sleep better, knowing that if you need anything, I'm not far away."

She hesitated, then nodded. He reached out his hand and pulled her to her feet, then handed her the crutch that would help keep her weight off her ankle for a few days.

"Come on," he said, wrapping his arm about her waist to support her. He kissed the side of her temple.

"How did I get so lucky with you?" she whispered.

The statement made his heart soar, but he knew the recovery from this trauma could take a while, and besides, he still didn't know what conclusions she'd come to at Ambrose.

By the time they reached his place, Amelia was half asleep. And even though she protested, he carried her into his condo and set her on the bed in his bedroom. He went about arranging her pillows, then covering her with a blanket.

"You're too good to me," Amelia said, reaching up to touch his face. "And I'm sorry about Hayden and what he did to you."

Grigg shook his head. "Don't worry about me, Mills." He stroked the side of her face, then kissed her other cheek.

Her eyes closed, and within moments she was asleep.

Still, Grigg sat in the chair opposite of the bed for a long time—watching over her and hoping that he'd never have to see Hayden's face again.

24

AMELIA OPENED HER eyes to the sound of heavy breathing. Her nightmarish dreams of Hayden driving her down endless dark roads morphed into the reality of a large Labrador retriever gazing at her, his face about three inches from her face.

"What did I tell you, Boomer?" Grigg said, coming around the corner. "Stay in the kitchen. Let her sleep—oh. You're awake." His voice softened, and he moved to her side.

Boomer relinquished his close-up position by a few inches.

"Sorry about that," Grigg said, looking her over. The bruising on his face was a deep purple now, darker than last night, but his eye was no longer swollen. "How are you feeling?"

She didn't know yet. Her throat was dry, and her stomach felt hollow. Oh, and her ankle throbbed, but all that was secondary to being safe now. "Okay, I guess."

At the raspy sound of her voice, Grigg produced a water bottle and some ibuprofen. "Here, take this. Breakfast will be ready in a few minutes. Spencer dropped Boomer off about an hour ago, and it was everything I could do to keep him from barking in excitement."

Amelia glanced at the dog. "I don't mind, huh, Boomer?"

Boomer took the mention of his name as a sign to move closer and nuzzle her face.

"That's enough, boy," Grigg said, physically moving Boomer out of the way.

Amelia didn't mind the dog's attention, but she was feeling rather weak. And surprisingly, starving. "What's for breakfast?"

Grigg smiled, and Amelia felt her heart tug.

"Hungry? I've got a surprise for you, then."

Just then a timer in the kitchen went off, and Grigg set the water bottle on the end table next to the bed. "Just a second. I'll bring you breakfast in bed."

"I can get up," Amelia said, but Grigg had already disappeared. So she relaxed her head against the pillow and glanced around the room. Grigg's bedroom. The honey-colored wooden blinds were shut, and the deep greens of the bedroom gave off a masculine yet calming feel. The pictures on the walls were of half-finished architectural plans. Interesting.

Something smelled good, and Amelia's stomach rumbled. Moments later, Grigg appeared with a tray of food. When he set it in front of her, Amelia said, "What is it?"

"The Edison special," he said, settling into the chair across from the bed. "My mom makes it on the weekends. Sort of like a casserole, but with hash browns, eggs, ham, and whatever else you want to add to it."

"Smells yummy," Amelia said, picking up her fork and scooping up a bite. Her gaze connected with Grigg's. "You going to watch me eat?"

He grinned. "I am."

Amelia laughed. Wow, it felt good to laugh. And with Grigg watching, she took a bite of his Edison special. "Delicious," she said after a moment of chewing. Then she took another bite.

Boomer whined, and Amelia gave him one of the bits of bacon.

"You just earned a friend for life," Grigg said.

She shrugged. "If he's your friend, then he's my friend." She gazed at Grigg for a moment. He looked relaxed in the chair, but the bruises on his face told a different story. He hadn't shaved, and he wore a well-washed T-shirt and gym shorts. She'd never seen him so dressed down before, but he looked sexy in whatever he wore. Her gaze returned to his bruised face. The guilt that surged up in her was hard to tamp down. Bringing Hayden back into her life had been a huge mistake. "I hope you can forgive me."

Grigg's brows pulled together. "For what?"

"For making that stupid list," she said, "and for putting Hayden on it."

Grigg rose and crossed to the bed. Sitting on the edge, facing her, he grasped her hand. "It's not your fault he's a horrible man. None of it was your fault. We were all deceived by him."

Amelia nodded, but that didn't dispel the lump in her throat. Grigg had told her about the break-in last night, and she knew they were both lucky that nothing worse had happened. "I hope he stays in jail for a long time."

Grigg drew her hand to his lips and pressed a kiss there. "He will. Don't worry."

The tenderness of Grigg's voice only made Amelia's eyes sting with emotion. She owed him so much. Not just for the past few hours but for all that he'd done for her, and meant to her, the past two years.

When a phone buzzed on the nightstand, she frowned. "Is that your phone?"

"Oh," Grigg said, unplugging the phone from the charger. "The cops located your phone and returned it."

"Wow. I'm impressed," she said.

Grigg handed her the phone. The thing was scratched up pretty good, and a long crack ran through the middle of the screen. But it worked for now.

There was also a text showing from Poppy.

"Did you . . . call my mom?" Amelia asked.

"No," he said, sounding surprised. "I let your grandmother know, since I'd already involved Shelton."

Amelia stared at the message on her phone. "She's in Denver. At my place."

Just then the phone rang. Poppy was calling, and Amelia answered it. "What are you doing at my place?" Perhaps it wasn't the nicest greeting, but Amelia was stunned.

"Millie?" Poppy said into the phone. "I've been so worried about you. When Gran told me what happened, I chartered a jet and flew to Denver. But where *are* you? I've been knocking and knocking. Did you go to *work*? You really should be taking the day off. Gran said you were kidnapped—"

"Mother," Amelia cut in. That word effectively sent Poppy into a shocked silence. "I'm not home, because I'm at Grigg's house. He's taking care of me."

Still no response from Poppy.

Amelia sighed. "I'll text you his address. You can come over."

"Oh, thank you, dear," Poppy gushed, having apparently found her voice. "I'll be there soon. You should see the flowers I picked out—"

"Bye," Amelia cut in. "Will text you the address." She hung up and closed her eyes. Without opening them, she said, "My mom's coming over."

"I heard," Grigg said, amusement in his tone. "Are you okay with that? Should I keep her occupied with Boomer?"

"She came all this way." Amelia opened her eyes. "You can let her in. I need to talk to her anyway." At the lift of Grigg's brows, she said, "But we need to talk first."

For the next few minutes, Amelia explained to Grigg how she'd come to the conclusion that she needed to first forgive her father. She told him about spending hours at his gravesite and then the experience of feeling his presence when she was with her grandma.

"Amazing," Grigg said at last. "You're amazing too."

Amelia pushed the tray farther aside and looped her arms about his neck. Grigg pulled her into a gentle hug, and as her heart beat with renewed warmth, she knew she could never let go of this man. Even working things out with her mother would be worth this prize in the end.

"So . . ." Grigg said against her neck. "Do you believe your grandma and what she said about how forgiving your mom would end the curse?"

"I do," Amelia said, her throat tightening up. "I can already feel a difference. The anger is leaving." She exhaled. "Do you think it will be enough?"

Grigg drew away enough to look her in the eyes. His hand rubbed slow circles on her back. "If it's not enough, then I'm still in, Mills. All the way in. No matter what."

Now tears did spill onto her cheeks.

Grigg lifted one of his hands and brushed away her tears with his thumb. Then he pressed his mouth softly against hers.

Amelia had quite enjoyed all of Grigg's kissing, whenever and wherever, but right now, right here, his soft kisses felt different somehow. As if they'd crossed some sort of invisible threshold of commitment.

She slid her hands through his hair and angled his mouth, wanting him to take things deeper. He complied, and her belly stirred with fire. In such a short time, this man had become her everything. And perhaps he had been for much longer than she thought.

His touch was gentle, caressing, but his kissing intensified, and she was becoming completely lost, crossing into another existence that centered around everything Grigg. Another existence that made all of her outside cares seem miniscule. Another existence that made even the curse fall away.

The doorbell rang, and it was like being doused with cold water. Because there was no way they could ignore this doorbell. It would be her mother.

Grigg smiled against Amelia's mouth, then kissed her one more time. "I'll get it," he whispered.

Then he let go of her, moved off the bed, and disappeared down the hall.

Amelia had only moments before she'd see her mother. If she wasn't ready now, then she'd never be. She smoothed the blanket over her legs and leaned back on the pillows. Maybe she should get up, but she could already hear her mother's voice as she came down the hall.

In predictable fashion, Poppy was dressed to the nines. Her ivory silk blouse was paired with a peach linen skirt that floated about her knees, and her diamond earrings had probably cost more than most people's cars.

"Oh, darling." Poppy moved to Amelia's side on silver stilettos. "You look awful." She leaned down and air-kissed Amelia.

Just because Amelia was working up the resolve to move past her mother's mistakes didn't mean they'd be best friends getting pedicures together. Amelia folded her arms. "You didn't have to come and check on me."

Poppy tilted her head. "You know, Millie, you're too pale. Maybe you should go out in the sun or try a tanning bed."

As usual, her mother was being ridiculous.

Grigg came in and picked up the tray. "Do you need anything else, Mills?"

Amelia knew what he was really asking—did he want her to stay? And the answer was yes. Whatever happened between her and her mom, Amelia needed his support. "Yes."

She didn't elaborate, and Grigg nodded. "I'll be right back."

While he was gone, Poppy crossed to the blinds and opened them. "This is a nice area, but really, Millie, you could do a lot better. You know, get into one of those gated communities."

"This isn't my place," Amelia said, holding back a groan of frustration.

"I know." Poppy whirled. "I was at your place, remember? It's cheap. Beneath an Ambrose, really."

Amelia gazed at her mother and her diamonds and dark lipstick and pencil-thin figure. Past the glamour and makeup, Amelia saw an emptiness. Like a black hole of nothing. A woman who had been trying to fill her life with possessions in order to replace her grief.

Grigg entered the room, and Amelia held out her hand, inviting him to sit by her. Which he did after making sure her foot was comfortably elevated.

Poppy watched the two of them, her lips pursed, her heavily lashed eyes taking in every movement.

"Mom," Amelia said. "Have a seat. We need to talk."

Lines appeared between Poppy's brows, something the Botox must have missed. "We *are* talking. Besides, I have a flight to catch soon. I can't be expected to change my entire schedule for whatever lecture you have in mind."

After a slow exhale, relying on the warmth of Grigg's fingers interlocked with hers, she said, "You chartered a jet, so I think you can sit down and hear me out."

Poppy's cheeks puffed, but she perched on the edge of the chair that Grigg had sat in earlier. She clasped her manicured fingers together, the multiple diamond rings catching the light from the sun coming through the blinds.

"I've been talking to Gran."

Poppy scoffed. "I'm sure you have. That woman is poisoning all of my daughters against me."

Amelia tightened her hold on Grigg's hand. "You should be more grateful, Mom."

This gave Poppy pause, and her non-Botoxed lines appeared again.

"*I'm* grateful," Amelia continued. "I'm grateful for Gran. I'm grateful to be an Ambrose woman. And I'm grateful for *you*."

Poppy visibly flinched. Amelia could see the conflicting emotions cross her mother's face, but she didn't give her a chance to respond before continuing.

"I've spent the last couple of days thinking about my childhood," Amelia said. "I know things between us weren't perfect, and our family dynamics were complicated, but I've reconciled myself to the fact that you were a good mother to me. You loved me, and you took care of me the best you could under hard circumstances. You were dealing with grief that I had no understanding of, and I was wrong to hold your pain against you."

Poppy blinked rapidly and looked toward the window, her hands clenched together in her lap.

"Mom, I'm truly sorry about your loss of your first husband," Amelia said in a quiet voice. "You were left a widowed mom, with three young girls who were grieving too. And then you trusted and loved again, married, and had me. Yet he left too. This time it was by choice, and I'm sure that was even more painful than becoming a widow. I'm so sorry for the additional pain my father caused you by leaving."

A single tear ran down the side of Poppy's cheek, but she still didn't meet Amelia's gaze. "You're too young to understand such things."

25

THE ONLY REASON Grigg remained in the room was because Amelia was gripping his hand.

He wasn't sure what to make of Poppy—she acted like a petulant teenager most of the time, but like Amelia, he'd sensed deep pain coming from the woman.

"I'm twenty-four, Mom," Amelia said, "but that's beside the point. You're right. I haven't been through what you've been through, and I can't truly understand. But I've had my own pain and struggles. I lost my father, twice. I was always second or third or fourth best in your life. I learned to live with that, and I learned to become my own strong woman. I have you to thank for that."

Poppy slowly turned her head and stared at Amelia. "You're . . . thanking me?"

"I am," Amelia confirmed with a nod. "If it weren't for the way you moved forward in your life, setting an example of how strong and stubborn Ambrose women are to the core, I would have been a crumpled mess."

A ghost of a smile lifted the edges of Poppy's mouth. "We Ambrose women are resilient, yes?"

Amelia smiled. "Yes."

Relief shot through Grigg. Maybe this discussion between mother and daughter would have a good outcome after all.

Poppy looked down at her hands. "I'd like to explain. Perhaps you *are* old enough to hear the truth."

Grigg ran his thumb over Amelia's fingers.

"Your father and I . . . things were rocky from the start," Poppy said. "Oh, we were infatuated with each other, as all couples are when they first start dating. He swept in with his charm and money and good looks. I finally felt pretty again. Valued. My girls adored him. We, uh, got pregnant, and of course he gallantly proposed. But sometimes the outside life with a single woman with three girls is much more complicated on the inside."

It sounded like Amelia's dad had been heroic, at least in the beginning.

"I was deathly ill during my pregnancy with you," Poppy said. "And truthfully, that was the beginning of the end. He took on the other girls, mind you, like a champ. But when I started feeling better, he would come home later and later at night. No, he wasn't having an affair. He just didn't want to deal with the chaos of the household."

Amelia released a breath. By the look on her face, Grigg knew that this was news to her.

"But my hopes were raised when you were born." Poppy offered a gentle smile. "Your father fell in love with you at first sight. He was home all the time after that. He walked the floors with you at night. He called during the day to find out how you were doing."

Amelia wiped at her own tears. At least this was good news, Grigg decided—her father had loved her deeply. But would this make the pain of abandonment harder?

"Our lives coasted along," Poppy continued. "We were happy for the most part. Yes, your father treated you like a princess and gallantly tolerated your half sisters. The divide increased between my girls as you grew older. He'd come to your preschool programs but miss other things of your sisters'. Sofia and Lauren noticed, of course. Emma was too young to voice any of it. But children aren't fools. I certainly didn't expect full equality, but I wanted him to be more present in my other daughters' lives, even if by half." She wiped at the new tears that had fallen on her cheeks. "You see, as a mother, loving your children is part of your soul. Their pain is your pain. I was hurting deeply, and I couldn't look beyond that. Day after day, it ate at me, until I finally confronted your father."

The room went silent, and Poppy rubbed her hands over her knees. "It was then that he confessed he had been seeing another woman for the past year." She took a shaky breath. "I was completely blindsided, probably because I'd been so wrapped up in raising four girls that I hadn't seen the signs. Or I'd just completely ignored them."

"I'm sorry," Amelia whispered. "I didn't know."

Poppy nodded. "No one knew. You're the first person I've told. You and Grigg." Her gaze connected with Grigg's.

He no longer saw a selfish, petulant woman in Poppy Ambrose. It was strange how opening one's heart could bring on a completely different perception. "Thank you for trusting me with your story."

Poppy exhaled. "I've been keeping it to myself for far too long. And it was wrong of me."

Amelia was busy wiping her own tears, so Grigg answered, "You were surviving the best you could. That's all anyone can ever be expected to do."

"Thank you for that, Grigg," Poppy said. "You're a good man." She looked down at her hands again. "Sometimes I've been impulsive in my dating and marrying habits. I suppose it's my own coping skill after losing the love of my life."

Grigg's heart ached at her words. Her pain was so palpable.

"But that still was no excuse to separate Millie from her father," Poppy said. "It's the greatest regret of my life." Her voice cracked, and she lifted her head to gaze at her daughter.

"Mine too," Amelia whispered.

"Can you ever forgive me, Millie?" Poppy asked.

Amelia sniffled, and neither woman spoke for a moment. "I already have, Mom," Amelia said at last.

Poppy's hand flew to her mouth. "Oh!" Then she moved to her feet in a flash and hurried to the bed, where she drew Amelia into her arms.

Amelia held onto her mother, and while both women cried and murmured unintelligible things, Grigg blinked back his own tears.

Poppy had been right. The Ambrose women were strong and courageous, and when it mattered most, they forgave each other and stuck together.

Moments later, Grigg had to chuckle when Poppy drew away, her makeup streaked along her face, and said, "Amelia Ambrose, you need a shower."

Then Poppy promptly turned to Grigg. "Lunch is on me. Now get dressed into something you can wear in public. You're a handsome man, and you should own it."

"Mo-om," Amelia said with a good-natured groan.

So it was, an hour later, they were all piled into Poppy's rented Mercedes, heading to a posh restaurant. According to Poppy, a simple sprained ankle shouldn't prevent her daughter from partaking in Denver's finest cuisine.

Amelia had protested that she wasn't even hungry, but Poppy quickly retorted, "I'm hungry, and I'm sure your man needs a decent meal, so think of someone else besides yourself."

The words might have sounded harsh to someone who didn't know Poppy, but Amelia only laughed.

Lunch with Poppy, to say the least, was an adventure. Grigg was completely fascinated by how she ordered, explaining down to the last minute detail how she wanted the parsley garnish arranged next to her chicken. But the best thing about the lunch was watching mother and daughter smile and tease each other. Even when they disagreed on something, which was every other topic, they argued good-naturedly.

But by the time they returned to his condo, Grigg could tell that Amelia was worn out. Boomer was only too happy to see everyone, and Grigg banished him to the back patio so Amelia could get some more rest. Poppy left in a flurry of hugs and air kisses, giving orders right and left to Amelia about making sure she ate healthy, got in the sun, didn't work too hard, started looking for a new place to live that was decent, and finally, took care of her man.

Which, of course, meant Grigg. And he was completely good with that.

When Grigg shut the door to his condo after he'd walked Poppy back to her car and waved her off, he felt like he'd lived two lifetimes.

"Hey," Amelia said from where she was sitting on the couch, her foot propped up on the coffee table.

Grigg turned. "Hey." Her smile was truly beautiful, made brighter by the weight that he knew had been lifted from her shoulders that morning. "Want some ice on that ankle?"

Amelia's smile remained. "Maybe later."

"What can I get you, then? Water? A pillow?"

"No," Amelia said in a soft voice. "I only want you."

Grigg's pulse hummed. "I think I can help with that."

Amelia gazed at him as he crossed the room and settled next to her. Slowly he threaded their fingers together, then drew her hand to his mouth and kissed each of her knuckles.

"I think things went well with my mom," Amelia said. "Don't you?"

Grigg met her eyes. "I think you're amazing, Amelia Ambrose."

Her lips quirked. "How amazing?"

He leaned forward, because it had been too long since he'd kissed her. She softened and welcomed him in. He pulled her as close as he was able, keeping in mind her injured ankle. She slid her hands up his chest, then behind his back, gripping the back of his shirt.

"It's going to be really hard returning to the office and not being able to kiss you when I want to," he whispered against her mouth.

"My office door locks," she whispered back.

He chuckled. "That's good to know." He ran his hands slowly down her back, then pressed his mouth against her jaw. "You need to take your time, you know, returning to work. I can handle things at the office for a while."

"Mmm," Amelia said. "We'll see."

"I'm serious," Grigg said, lifting his head.

She only smiled, which only made Grigg want to kiss her again, so he did.

"I think I'm addicted to you, Mills," he murmured.

"That's a good thing," she said. "Because I think the curse is broken, which means that you're number one on my list."

"Last man standing, huh?" he teased.

"Yep."

"Well, that's good news," he said, holding her gaze. "Because I'm in love with you, and I don't ever want to let you go."

Amelia's eyes widened slightly, then her mouth curved upward. "What about the curse?"

"What curse?" Grigg asked.

The smile spread across her face. "You sound pretty confident, Mr. Edison."

"Oh, I am, Miss Ambrose," Grigg said. "Besides, should I meet an untimely death, I'll die happy, knowing that every day leading up to it I spent with you."

"Sounds like you have big plans."

"Oh, I do," Grigg said with a grin. "And the first plan is to kiss you senseless. Then you're going to take a nap while I sort out a few work details."

"Are you going to update the Lampton's Furniture spreadsheet?" she asked.

"I am," he said. "I need to put in a few scenarios for Lampton to consider before we agree to fund their new upgrades."

"Oh, I like it when you talk numbers," she said. "Kind of sexy. Makes me love you even more."

"Even more?" he prompted, unable to keep the smile off his face.

"That's what I said." She moved her fingers along his jaw, and Grigg was pretty sure his entire body had broken out in goose bumps. "I love you, Grigg, and I'm sorry it took me so long to work out the mess of my life."

He captured her fingers in his hand. "You were worth every minute of waiting."

She smiled, then her blue eyes searched his. "Now, weren't you going to kiss me senseless?"

"Yes," Grigg said. So that's exactly what he did.

Heather B. Moore is a four-time *USA Today* bestselling author. She writes historical thrillers under the pen name H.B. Moore; her latest thrillers include *The Killing Curse* and *Breaking Jess*. Under the name Heather B. Moore, she writes romance and women's fiction. Her newest releases include the contemporary sports romances, Belltown Six Pack series, and the small town romance series, Pine Valley. She's also one of the coauthors of the *USA Today* bestselling series: Timeless Romance Anthologies. Heather writes speculative fiction under the pen name Jane Redd; releases include the Solstice series, *Mistress Grim* and *Midsummer Night*. Heather is represented by Dystel, Goderich & Bourret.

For book updates, sign up for Heather's email list:
hbmoore.com/contact
Amazon Author Page: Heather B. Moore
Website: HBMoore.com
Facebook: Fans of H. B. Moore
Blog: MyWritersLair.blogspot.com
Instagram: @authorhbmoore
Twitter: @HeatherBMoore

www.ingramcontent.com/pod-product-compliance
Lightning Source LLC
LaVergne TN
LVHW021819060526
838201LV00058B/3445